The Christmas Cantata

A St. Germaine Christmas Entertainment

Mark Schweizer

SJMP<u>BOOKS</u>

Liturgical Mysteries
by Mark Schweizer

Why do people keep dying in the little town of St. Germaine, North Carolina? It's hard to say. Maybe there's something in the water. Whatever the reason, it certainly has *nothing* to do with St. Barnabas Episcopal Church!

Murder in the choirloft. A choir-director detective. They're not what you expect...they're even funnier!

The Alto Wore Tweed
The Baritone Wore Chiffon
The Tenor Wore Tapshoes
The Soprano Wore Falsettos
The Bass Wore Scales
The Mezzo Wore Mink
The Diva Wore Diamonds
The Organist Wore Pumps
The Countertenor Wore Garlic
The Christmas Cantata
The Treble Wore Trouuble

Now available at
your favorite mystery bookseller or
sjmpbooks.com.

"It's like Mitford meets Jurassic Park, only without the wisteria and the dinosaurs ..."

Advance Praise for *The Christmas Cantata*

"An obvious rip-off of *MY* new book—*The Christmas Shotgun*—but go ahead and read it anyway."
Sarah Palin, celebritition

"Sweet as possum pie."
Linda Edwards Campbell, actress

"This is the best Christmas story since the 1978 *Star Wars Holiday Special*."
Ryan Buss, son-in-law

"I read this book at the library. It was so good that I asked God for my own copy, but I know God doesn't work that way so I stole the book and asked for forgiveness."
Name Withheld, chaplain, KA (Kleptomaniacs Anonymous)

"Does this book smell like chloroform to you?"
Margaret Secour, choir director

"The voices in Schweizer's head may not be real, but they have some very good ideas."
Peter Hawes, retired priest

"The perfect 'read' while you're stuck in the blood-pressure machine down at the Piggly Wiggly."
Pam McNeil, pianist

"The book that put the 'Oo' in book!"
Jeff McLelland, organist and choir director

"Buy this book immediately! Then send an email to the first ten people on your email list and tell them to buy it as well. In thirty days you will have 17 million dollars. I don't know how it works—it just *does!* But whatever you do, don't break the chain. My cousin did and she not only lost the money, but Mr. Sniffles came to a terrible end (the cat, not the butler)."
Anne Porter, recent millionaire

"If you never read another book, this should be it."
Richard Shephard, Chamberlain, York Minster

The Christmas Cantata
A St. Germaine Christmas Entertainment
Copyright ©2011 by Mark Schweizer

Published by
SJMP<u>BOOKS</u>
www.sjmpbooks.com
P.O. Box 249
Tryon, NC 28782

ISBN 978-0-9844846-9-0

Poems by Sara Teasdale (1884-1933)
Stars (1920)
Barter (1917)
The Kiss (1915)

Acknowledgements
Nancy Cooper, Beverly Easterling, Betsy Goree,
Donald Hawthorne, Kristen Linduff, Beth McCoy,
Mary J. Miller, Patricia Nakamura, Donis Schweizer,
Liz Schweizer, Richard Shephard, Holly D. Wallace,
and Barbara Cawthorne Crafton

Chapter 1

November, 1937

She had just returned from Paris. It had been a grueling journey, although the sea voyage hadn't been too bad, taking a little over a week to make the crossing from Le Havre to New York. Her father had booked her passage on the S.S. Normandie, the flagship of the French line Compagnie Générale Trans-atlantique. Only two years old, the ship was a marvel, the most powerful steam turboelectric powered vessel ever built. Even so, she had found the passage trying. Following her arrival in New York, she'd boarded a train, then another, then yet another, before disembarking in Asheville for the car trip home.

The young woman had departed for Europe two years earlier on the Graf Zeppelin, a luxury afforded to her by her father after her graduation from Asheville Normal and Teacher's College, but to return on a zeppelin was out of the question. Not after what happened to the Hindenburg the previous May.

The old railroad man required that his daughter get a teaching degree. Study in music was not an option. She had swallowed her disappointment and struck a deal with her father. She'd get her teaching certificate, but then be allowed to travel in Europe for two years after its completion. She promised her parents that she would visit many countries and that it would broaden her horizons. It wasn't an odd request for the time. Many young people headed to Europe and other exotic venues in the gap between education and settling into adulthood.

5

She was never in want of money during her excursion. The family was well off, Father having been employed his entire career by the Vanderbilts, and he didn't hold onto the purse strings too tightly where his little girl was concerned. He would be eulogized many years later as a doting father and husband, a good businessman, and someone who put his daughter's welfare above all else. This was the truth. Why else would he have insisted on the best piano teachers in western North Carolina from the time she was six years old? Why else would he have made sure she spoke French, German, and a little Italian? Why else would he have put his foot down and guided her away from music and toward the teaching profession when it became clear that she wanted to have a career? Better a teacher than a secretary, or worse, an itinerant musician, he said.

She was as good as her word and did, in fact, travel across the continent of Europe for the first two months, visiting many countries. Then, feeling the need for a home-base, she'd settled in Paris and, on a whim, applied for a job playing piano for a few evenings a week at Maison Prunier on Avenue Victor Hugo. Although jazz was all the rage, the owner of the restaurant was an aficionado of Mozart, and she knew all but one of the boy genius' eighteen piano sonatas from memory. It was on one of those evenings that she met Nadia Boulanger.

It was actually a woman named Annette Dieudonné who approached the piano after the girl played the final chords of one of her favorites: Number 18, the one in D major. Mozart's last.

"You play beautifully," Annette said in perfect English. "We understand from our waiter that you are an American. My friend would like to meet you. Nadia Boulanger? Perhaps you know of her? Would you care to join us?"

The young woman's heart skipped a beat. Of course she had heard of Nadia Boulanger: student of Fauré and Widor, friend of Stravinsky and Dukas, teacher of Aaron Copland, Roy Harris, Virgil Thomson, and a host of others. Of course she would like to join them. Of course, of course!

She spent the next half hour answering questions. What was her name? (She answered "Elle" even though it was not. Her own name, she suddenly decided, was too pedestrian, too American.) How did you come to be in Paris? Where are you staying? With whom have you studied? Gerard Aguillon? Gerard is one of my dearest friends! In North Carolina, you say? Composition as well as piano? I knew he was in America, but Asheville of all places. I thought I recognized the phrasing in the Adagio! Oh, don't take offense, my dear! It takes years to find your voice and you are still a baby. Did you know that Elle is my cousin's name? You simply must come to supper!

The next twenty-two months were spent in blissful study: traditional harmony, score reading at the piano, species counterpoint, analysis, and finally, composition. "You need an established language," Mademoiselle Boulanger told her. "Then, within that established language, you will discover the liberty to be yourself. It is always necessary to be yourself – that is a mark of genius."

She didn't tell her father what she was doing, but she secretly wrote and told her mother everything.

St. Germaine, North Carolina, was in a crabby mood. Yes, the whole town. If a temperament could affect an entire populace, "crabby" was what St.

Germaine was. Noylene's new personal astrologer, a woman named Goldi Fawn Birtwhistle, blamed it on the convergence of Pluto and the third moon of Jupiter.

Goldi Fawn was a hair professional and the latest to join the cast at the Beautifery, Noylene Fabergé-Dupont-McTavish's Oasis of Beauty. Goldi Fawn was a woman of generous proportions with an unknown complexion for whom the word "pancake" obviously had multiple and disparate connotations. She would freely admit that she wasn't as adept with make-up as she was with hair, but, as she liked to point out to her customers, her own hair was her "crowning glory." The color was Medium Champagne Blonde No. 3 and it sat piled high on her head with untamed wisps dangling down in what Goldi Fawn described as her come-hither "Delilah" look.

"First Corinthians 11:15," she'd say to whomever was sitting in her chair. "A woman's hair is her crowning glory and I oughta know. I had my own hair studio in Johnson City. You're *from* Johnson City? Well, you know that liquor store by the railroad tracks next to the Righteous Arm of God Pentecostal Holiness Church of the Redeemer? You do? Well, right behind that liquor store was where I had my studio. It was called Crowning Glory Hairstyles. That's right! I don't mind advertising my faith wherever I can. Lookee here. I've even got a Jesus Fish on my hair dryer ..."

Goldi Fawn saw no problem in combining the Christian faith and astrology. "God made the stars, and it's my spiritual gift to understand what they have to say to us."

The resulting exchange was inevitable. "Astrology is of the devil," Darla would say. Darla was one chair over and another of the licensed Women of Beauty whose mission was to offer glamour and allurement to the needy females of St. Germaine.

"There will be signs in the sun, moon, and stars," Goldi Fawn would reply, using one of the many scripture references at her disposal thanks to her penchant for writing them on slips of paper with various colored markers and thumb-tacking them to the wall around her station. "Just lookit," she'd say, pointing to one of her Bible verses. "It's right there in Luke 21:25. And I won't even mention the fact that the wise men from the east, the ones looking for the baby Jesus were ..." she paused for effect ... "yes, I believe I'm correct in saying this ... *astrologers*." She'd give a self-satisfied smile while she smeared some color onto a piece of tinfoil. "Or are you going to tell me I am mistaken? I can show you several scholastic references if you're interested. And I have many other scriptures you might like to consider."

"I'll give you a scripture," Darla would mutter under her breath, all the while eyeing her sharpest pair of scissors resting on the counter. "Thou shalt not suffer a witch to live."

According to Goldi Fawn, the aforementioned heavenly convergence was responsible for the attitude of the entire town, and that attitude—make no mistake—was "crabby." Pete Moss, owner of the Slab Café, thought that the crabbiness might have something to do with the increased bombardment of positive ions from outer space; these ions funneled directly toward St. Germaine. Also included in Pete's theory were sunspots, an ever-widening hole in the ozone layer, the federal deficit, armadillo migration, and the cancellation of two long-running soap operas. "My God ... Erica," he'd say, close to tears, his face buried in his hands. "What will I do without Erica?"

9

Usually, in St. Germaine, the three weeks before Christmas were marked by an increase in good feelings toward one's fellow man.

Not this year.

St. Germaine is our small village situated in the Appalachian Mountains in northwest North Carolina. There is a downtown square that gives structure to the town's layout and in the center of the square is Sterling Park; a couple of acres of grass; seasonal flower beds; large maple, poplar, and chestnut trees; a white gazebo; and a statue of Harrison Sterling, the mayor who, in 1961, talked the city council into retaining all of the downtown edifices by way of levying hefty fines on those owners intent on embracing the then-current trend of slapping aluminum siding on everything, or, even worse, tearing it down and replacing it with "modern architecture." Since it was financially disastrous for the merchants to tear down their stores or cover them up, they restored them instead. The result was a mixture of quaint and beautiful buildings surrounding the park.

The largest building on the square—the nineteenth-century courthouse—anchored the structures on the east side. The police station stood adjacent, and shops and eating establishments were nestled side by side around the square like a full-sized Dicken's village. The next largest (and the newest) building was St. Barnabas Episcopal Church, which looked almost directly across the park at the courthouse. Although the church was only a few years old, the architect and the builders had replicated the facade of the old church, the one lost in a terrible fire, down to the last detail, even going so far as to source the stone from the same quarry as the original structure. Besides the church, the St. Germaine Downtown Association membership included the Slab Café, Schrecker's Jewelry, the Bear and Brew, a flower boutique, the Ginger Cat, Eden Books, the Appalachian Music Shoppe, the library, Holy Grounds (our Christian Coffee emporium), Noylene's Beautifery, several lawyers' offices, and a handful of antique and mountain-crafty stores.

St. Germaine is dependent on the tourist trade. We have tourists in the summer who are trying to escape the heat of Florida, Georgia, and even South Carolina. They stay from mid-June through August. The next batch comes into town for leaf season around the second week of October and they come by the thousands. Leaf season (when the leaves change from green to their autumn hues and the foliage is at its most beautiful) lasts for about four weeks, give or take. The five bed and breakfasts in town are booked months and sometimes years in advance. Then, starting at Thanksgiving, the throngs begin their thronging on the weekends. Closer to Christmas, these visitors extend their stay for a few days on either end and the town is packed.

The principal reason for their migration is shopping, but that isn't the only draw. St. Germaine offers something that can't be found in many other places. The Germans have a word for it: *Gemütlichkeit*. Its closest English equivalent is the word "coziness," however, rather than merely describing a place that is compact, well-heated, or nicely furnished (a cozy room for example), *Gemütlichkeit* connotes the notion of belonging, social acceptance, well-being, cheerfulness, the absence of anything hectic, and the opportunity to spend quality time with friends and family. This is St. Germaine during the Christmas season.

From Thanksgiving weekend through New Year's Day, downtown St. Germaine is decorated as if Martha Stewart had gone on a holiday rampage. The park, storefronts, streetlights, abandoned cars, trees, bushes, and everything else—nailed down or not—are festooned with pine and fir garlands, tens of thousands of lights, ribbons, wreaths, and ornaments of every size and description. One year Nancy Parsky, my lieutenant, even found a dead turtle (she surmised by the smell that it had met its end sometime in October) lying in the gutter with a red bow stuck to its shell and a blinking Rudolph nose tied to its head. And decorating is just the cinnamon on the eggnog.

It is the town's mission to make everyone feel welcome. From the oldest resident to the newest, locals and visitors, tourists and shoppers, all are gladly and warmly received. Shopping in St. Germaine doesn't have that hurried, frantic feeling that the malls and the mega-stores seem to produce. Yes, we have lines, but if you find yourself having to wait in one, someone will be happy to chat with you, any number of people will wish you a Merry Christmas and offer to hold your packages for a while, or an employee might walk up and give you a cup of hot chocolate and a hug. If you can't find something for that special someone on your shopping list, the owner of the store might suggest you try the Ginger Cat down the street, or even call into Blowing Rock because she saw "just the thing you're looking for" the last time she was shopping there.

Is all this goodwill an accident of geography or maybe a Brigadoon-like aberration? It is not. It is a well-thought-out, careful plan instituted about fifteen years earlier by Pete Moss, the mayor of St. Germaine at the time. Pete saw it as a cross between *It's a Wonderful Life* and *Field of Dreams*, telling the city council that people were longing for small town America and "if we build it, they will come." It took a few years to implement Pete's plan—to get everyone on board—but once started, the goodwill was self-perpetuating, and it didn't take long for word to get around.

St. Germaine has added various Christmas events over the years to keep things fresh; the outdoor Living Nativity presented in alternate years by either the Kiwanis or Rotary Club, rival civic organizations; the Christmas Parade, hosted by the club that *isn't* in charge of the Nativity; and, last year, the St. Lucy Walk on December 13th in support of acid-reflux research. This was an idea that Vernell Lombard, a newly-elected member of the city council, had come up with. Her husband, Buddy, had just been told by his doctor that his heartburn was most probably caused by acid reflux.

"Why doesn't he just stop eatin' like a hog?" asked Cynthia Johnsson, the current mayor, when Vernell brought the proposal in front of the council at their September meeting. "I waited on him down at the Slab Café and he put away half a dozen chili dogs, a large order of onion rings, potato salad, and two slabs of apple pie." Cynthia, in addition to her part-time job as mayor, was a professional waitress and belly dancer. Usually Cynthia was well-spoken and used the King's English albeit with a slight North Carolina accent, but when she "got in thar amongst 'em," as she said, her dialect dropped right into the vernacular of the rest of the city council. "I saw Buddy tear through that food like a human garbage disposal. If he'd stopped to take a breath, one of

13

them six wieners might have stood a fighting chance."

"Acid reflux is a disease," said Vernell, her mouth set in a hard line. "Like brain cancer, or erectile disfunction. There just *has* to be more research. Anyway, Buddy was in a hurry. He's only got a half hour for lunch. Let's vote on it."

"Fine," said Cynthia, throwing her hands into the air with the realization that she'd never get the forty-five minutes back the council had just spent arguing about the project.

"Fine," she repeated. "Let's vote."

In the end, the vote was five to four in favor of the project and the St. Lucy Walk was scheduled and well publicized. St. Lucy isn't so much remembered for suffering from acid reflux as she is for having her eyes removed and served up on a plate just prior to her head being cut off, but St. Lucy's Day was in December—December 13th to be exact—and would fit in well with the St. Germaine Christmas celebration scheme. St. Lucy's Day is now most often celebrated in the Scandinavian countries by young girls dressed in white who walk through the town wearing a crown of lit candles on their heads. Once Vernell discovered *that* little tidbit, she invited all the girls in town between the ages of twelve and twenty-one to participate, provided they could supply their own white gown and bring their own candles. It was a very beautiful sight and we had quite a large turnout, not only among the girls who were happy to march in support of a worthy cause, but also the folks who dropped coins into their red velvet purses—purses that Vernell had made the night before—as they walked along their route.

The fund-raiser went as smoothly as could be expected. That is to say that only two of the girls lit their hair on fire and had to be doused by the chaperones standing on each corner of the square brandishing CO_2 fire extinguishers. No one was seriously hurt, although there was talk at the Beautifery that wigs might be needed all the way through Groundhog Day. Vernell blamed the accidents on Noylene who was in charge of coiffing the girls for the event. "That Noylene uses too much hairspray!" she said. "Them girls was walkin' fire-bombs."

The St. Lucy Walk raised $232.45 and Vernell promised to write a check and send it to the Society for the Movement toward Acid Reflux Prevention (SMARP), headquartered in Pascagoula, Mississippi. The prevailing thought, though, was that Buddy spent the money on hot dogs.

The council had decided not to sponsor the St. Lucy Walk this year, but the Living Nativity (it was the Rotarians' turn) had been scheduled for the third week in December, and the Christmas Parade (this year hosted by the Kiwanians) was always a big hit. The economy was better than it had been for a couple of years. People were pouring into town and goodwill and friendliness should have been the order of the day. But this year was different. This year, St. Germaine was just plain crabby.

Chapter 2

It was a Monday, and there were exactly three weeks until Christmas. As the choir director and organist at St. Barnabas, this concerned me. In my capacity as the police chief of St. Germaine, I was less concerned, but at this time of year it was not difficult to let the one responsibility slide in deference to the other.

I'd been the chief for nineteen years, ever since I'd been hired by Pete Moss, the then-recently-elected mayor of St. Germaine who had found himself in need of a constabulary officer. Detective Hayden Konig, Chief of Police: that's what my card said. I'd been the musician at the church for almost as long as I'd been the chief, although I'd taken the occasional hiatus. I had a Master's degree from UNC in music and another one in criminology. This, apparently, gave me all kinds of credibility in both fields. I could spot a French 6th chord or a double-parked car with equal proficiency.

Pete's primary occupation, now that he was no longer the mayor (which didn't pay that much anyway), was to be the purveyor of "fine dining" at the Slab Café. "Fine dining" might be a stretch, but if you asked any local about the food at the Slab, they'd say, "Oh, it's fine." It was enough for Pete to slap the motto on the front of the menu. In fact, the Slab served a great breakfast; sandwiches, burgers, and just good all-around lunch fare; and had a pie case full of homemade desserts.

I was sitting at our "designated" table (reserved for the SGPD and friends) in the Slab Café at seven in the morning. I expected Nancy to join me shortly. Dave wouldn't make it into the office until nine or so.

There were three other customers in the restaurant. I didn't recognize them.

When I first came to St. Germaine, I comprised the entire police force. Now we numbered three: myself, Nancy Parsky, and Dave Vance. Nancy was a great cop. Dave was great at filling out reports and running errands for Nancy. He was also in charge of donut procurement.

"What do you want?" said Pete from behind the counter. I could tell he was not in a good mood. Crabby. "Noylene will be here in a bit. She just called in. Frozen pipes." Pete, unlike the rest of the folks in the Slab, was dressed in a Hawaiian shirt and jeans. He'd given up his flip-flops once the health department complained. Still, in essence a hippie from the seventies, he now tied his gray hair in a ponytail and only wore his earring on days that started with a "T."

"Just coffee right now," I answered.

"Get it yourself, will you?" Pete crabbed.

"Oh, sure," I answered as snarkily as I could. "Don't worry about it. Allow *me!*" If Pete noticed my sarcasm, he ignored it.

The coffee station was at the end of the counter and Pete had a couple of full pots resting on warmers and another one brewing. In front of the counter were four stools, one of them occupied by a man with his wool cap pulled down over his ears. The other two customers were men as well, both in the insulated coveralls that marked them as utility workers. They sat across from each other in one of the six booths that lined one of the walls. The tables, mine included, were covered with red and green checkered vinyl tablecloths and decorated with a few Christmas ornaments. There were colored holiday lights strung throughout the café, and Noylene had put some of her "signature" homemade Christmas

17

wreaths up on the wall, along with the prices, just in case someone might like one for their home.

Noylene was a woman of many talents. Along with waiting tables at the Slab and being the owner of the Beautifery, she also ran the Dip-n-Tan, a contraption by which anyone with $24.95 could be lowered, naked, into a vat of tanning fluid and generally come out looking like they'd just spent a week in the Caribbean. If the formula was slightly off, though, as it frequently was in the early days of the Dip-n-Tan, a customer might end up a lovely shade of pumpkin. Noylene had taken to testing the formula before dipping a nervous customer by lowering a pig head into the vat, leaving it there for two minutes, then pulling it out and comparing it to a chart she'd fixed to the wall. She'd gotten so she could gauge the strength of the tanning fluid pretty well and pig heads were free since she'd made that bartering deal with Jenny Limpet, the butcher's wife. She traded professional beautifying in exchange for pig heads, and she had a freezer full. A bonus was that she could sell the heads, after they'd been organically tanned, to a restaurant specializing in Scottish cuisine, where her son, D'Artagnan Fabergé, worked as a sous chef.

"Noylene say how many of her pipes burst?" I asked.

"She didn't know," grumbled Pete. "She told me D'Artagnan was coming over to crawl under the house and check."

"It's a wonder mine didn't bust," said the man at the counter. "Five degrees last night. Who ever heard of weather like this so early in December?"

"I remember the same thing back in '89," said one of the utility workers. "It was eleven below zero. I remember because it was my first year on the job. I've never been so cold."

"At least we ain't gettin' snow," said his companion. He got up to refill his coffee cup.

"Too cold for snow," said the man at the counter. He took a loud, slow slurp of his own coffee. "Supposed to drop down even lower tonight."

"Sheesh," said Pete. "That's too dang cold. I don't care how Christmasy the town is. Nobody's coming in to shop if it's below zero outside."

The cowbell tied to the inside of the door banged noisily against the glass and Cynthia Johnsson came into the restaurant, smacking her gloved hands together, trying to get some feeling back into her numbed fingers.

"You should have called me," she said to Pete. She peeled off her gloves, then took off her coat and scarf and hung them on one of the hooks that lined the wall beside the door. "Noylene sent me a text. Her pipes are broken."

"Yeah, I know," said Pete. "I just didn't want to wake you." His tone softened for the first time since I'd come in. "Thanks for coming in, though."

Cynthia and Pete had been a couple since Cynthia defeated Pete in a hotly-contested mayoral election a few years ago. Pete, a two-time loser in the marriage department, was magnanimous in defeat and showed no animosity at all, preferring now to be the power behind the throne. "I'm not saying that Cynthia's a puppet ruler," he told me. "I'm just saying that a lot of ideas get tossed around under the covers after the town council has gone to bed."

Cynthia walked behind the counter, gave Pete a peck on the cheek and donned her half-apron. She reached under the counter and came up with a book, then walked over to the table.

"I brought this in yesterday," she said. "I don't know if you might want it or not, but I found it in one of the file boxes in the basement of the courthouse. I don't think anyone's been through that stuff for thirty years."

"I can guarantee it," said Pete. "I was just gonna throw it all in the dumpster about ten years ago, but then I forgot."

"Anyway," continued Cynthia, "the state says everything is going digital, so we have to scan all the records and whatever else is lying around, including Pete's expense vouchers for the past twenty years."

"*What?*" said Pete. "Hang on ... that stuff's classified!"

Cynthia ignored him. "We were clearing out the papers we didn't need, and found this." She handed me the book. "It has nothing to do with city business, so just throw it away if you don't want it."

The book was oversized, about ten inches by sixteen, and had a blank hardboard cover and stitched binding. The title page announced *La Chanson d'Adoration* by Elle de Fournier, not a composer I knew. I flipped to a random page and perused the hand-copied music manuscript, beautifully done. I knew the look. This was a performance score, notated by one of any number of copyists working in New York City when classical musicians could supplement their meager income by putting composers' scrawl into legible form. This was done in the days before computers had taken over the music engraving business, or even before copy machines. I turned back to the beginning of the score.

"So what do you think?" asked Cynthia.

"I'll look at it, but to be honest, most of this kind of stuff isn't worth the time and money it took to have it transcribed. It most probably got one performance, if that, and was relegated to the composer's resumé."

"Well, whatever," said Cynthia. "I thought you'd like to see it."

"Thanks," I said. "I really will give it a look. You never know."

The cowbell clanged again and Nancy came in, mimicking the hand slapping that Cynthia had just gone through.

"Man, it's cold," she said, unbundling.

"Not my fault," said Pete.

"Never said it was," snapped Nancy.

Nancy Parsky was dressed, as she always was when she was on duty, in her police uniform—standard issue dark brown pants and khaki shirt, this one long-sleeved. Her badge was prominently displayed and her gun was holstered high on her hip. She had on her law enforcement issue parka and a trapper style hat of muskrat fur and leather that made its appearance whenever the temperature dropped below ten degrees or so. Lieutenant Parsky had picked this one up on one of her summer trips to Canada and, although she didn't care for hats and usually didn't wear one, the bitter cold made almost everyone, including Nancy, forsake fashion for comfort.

"Who's making breakfast?" Nancy asked. "Is Manuel here?"

"Nope," said Pete. "His car wouldn't start. I'm cooking a breakfast casserole. Eggs, spicy sausage, bread, cheese ... It's Manuel's recipe. He read it to me over the phone. It'll be ready in five minutes."

"Figures," said Nancy. "Pete's home cooking. It's gonna be another one of those days. Well, bring it on I suppose." The skepticism was evident in her voice. Since Manuel had taken over the kitchen a few months earlier, culinary expectations had risen dramatically.

"We're all hoping for the best," said the man at the counter.

"Hey!" said Pete, "if you guys don't like it ..."

"Everyone calm down," said Cynthia. "What's going on here? It's like this all over town."

"Crabby Christmas," I said. "Happens every once in a while."

"Positive ion bombardment," said Pete, as if this explained everything. "Or maybe sunspots. Sorry I snapped. It'll pass."

Nancy walked to the coffee machine, poured herself a cup, then sat down next to me.

"You're up early this morning," she said.

"Well, I had to get up and run five miles. I figured after that, why not come into work?"

"Five miles?" said Nancy. "Really?"

"Of course not," I grumbled. "You think I'm one of those crazy people who runs five miles when it's a few degrees above zero? You could die out there! Nope. I've gone back to my expando-pants for the winter. I'm just hoping to gain only fifteen pounds between now and New Year's Day."

"Huh," said Nancy. "I'm not sure I can respect a man who wears maternity clothes, even if it is five degrees outside."

"Expando-pants!" I said, putting my thumb into my waistband and giving them a tug. "Look, they have these side gussets."

"Yeah, yeah," said Nancy. "Well, I ran *my* five miles." She picked up the music manuscript. "What's this?"

"Some music Cynthia found in a box in the basement of the courthouse."

"Is it worth anything?" asked Nancy. Nancy was a fan of *Antiques Roadshow*.

"I doubt it, but I'm going to give it a look."

"Well, who's the composer?" Nancy already had her iPhone out and was busy bringing up her Google page.

"Elle de Fournier." I pushed the book, opened to the title page, across the table. Nancy checked the spelling, typed the information in, and shrugged her shoulders a moment later.

"Nope," she said. "There are a couple *Elisabeth* de Fourniers, but none that look like composers."

"I didn't think there would be," I said. "I'll play through it though. Maybe there's something in it worth excerpting."

"Hang on," said Nancy. She'd turned the title page and was now looking at the verso side where a quarter sheet of folded, lined paper was glued into the binding. She unfolded the paper gently, taking care not to pull it loose. "Look here," she said. "Premiered at St. Barnabas Church, Christmas Eve, 1942."

"Really?"

She spun the book around and pushed it back across the table. The inscription was in faded red pencil, but easily read.

"Interesting," I said.

"Maybe you can check the church records," said Cynthia, looking over my shoulder. "There's got to be some mention of it somewhere. A bulletin maybe."

"All the church records were burned up in the fire three years ago," I said. "Bulletins, baptisms, weddings, old pictures, the whole lot. Someone might remember singing it ..."

"I doubt it," said Cynthia. "That was over sixty years ago. I can't remember the sermon I heard last week."

"How about the newspaper?" asked Nancy. "I mean, this was a premiere performance. Certainly newsworthy."

"The *St. Germaine Tattler* didn't even exist until 1950," said the man at the counter. "There was a paper in the '20s. Another in the '30s and '40s. Both long closed and out of business. The *Watauga Democrat* might have something, though."

We all looked over at him. He shrugged and splayed his hands. "What?" he said. "I work for the *Democrat*. Over in Boone. You want me to check on it for you?"

"That'd be great," I said, and watched him scribble the information on a napkin.

"No old copies anywhere?" Pete said. "Of the St. Germaine papers, I mean."

"Not that I know of," answered the newspaperman. "I don't even remember the names of those old rags."

"Even if it wasn't in one of the newspapers," I said, folding the notation back into the position in which Nancy had discovered it, "some people have long memories."

Premiered at St. Barnabas Church, Christmas Eve, 1942.

Chapter 3

She'd met Henry Greenaway at her twenty-sixth birthday party in September, 1941. She hadn't given the tall, bespectacled, thoughtful man a second look when her cousin Emily first introduced him to their circle of friends. Emily, it seemed, had her cap set for Henry and clung to him like a treed possum, although he appeared indifferent to her coquettish behavior. She was no classic beauty, unless one tended to favor a female with an equine countenance. Emily was said to bear a striking resemblance to Eleanor Roosevelt, but unlike Eleanor, she had quite a figure and, if rumors carried any truth to them, was determined that potential suitors would remember her for her other attributes rather than for her horse-like features. Her Seabiscuit face, accentuated with a dental configuration that allowed her to win each and every "bobbing for apples" competition she'd ever entered, was framed by a mane of peroxide-white hair, but if a young man could focus his attention below her clavicles, he would find her to be very attractive. And willing. Yes, very willing indeed.

Early in the evening Emily had managed to fall into the swimming pool and, since she hadn't brought a change of clothes, remained in her wet, clinging, white silk charmeuse dress until the chill of the autumn air was too much for her to bear and she donned a full-length mink coat that just happened to be in the trunk of her car. Henry had gallantly offered her his tweed jacket after she had fallen in, but she had refused it repeatedly, preferring the warmth of the stares of the other young gentlemen at the party. The other girls were not amused.

One of the gawkers—really, who could blame him—was her own date, Rod Fontineau, a baseball player who played for the Asheville Tourists. She had no patience for such shenanigans, and soon gravitated to the quiet, introspective fellow who seemed unfazed by Emily's antics and obvious lack of undergarments. They sat by the pool, sipped summer wine, and discussed various topics including literature and poetry, two subjects that had always managed to stump poor Rod, while the rest of the party danced far into the night.

Henry had asked her out that very evening just before bundling a very inebriated Emily into her car, getting behind the wheel, and driving her home. During the weeks that followed, she'd discovered that Henry was a Yale grad and that his interest in music and poetry was well and truly grounded. He'd double-majored in English literature and business and, although he had no formal musical training, he'd sung with the Yale Glee Club for four years and had, in fact, been one of the Whiffenpoofs.

It was April when he proposed. April, 1942. They'd talked about their future together and she was over the moon when he practically begged her to give up her teaching job and go back to her first love, music. Money would not be a problem, he'd said. With a job waiting for him in the family business, they had a life to look forward to. He'd be back home in just a few months, a year at most.

They married at the Asheville courthouse, much to her mother's dismay. Two weeks later he shipped off to the Army's 18th Infantry and left for North Africa.

"What are you playing?" asked Meg. I was in the den, seated at the grand piano, doing my best to read the open score which included two bassoons, oboe doubling on English horn, flute, clarinet, and organ. The den was an original log cabin and, if the sketchy provenance I'd been provided meant anything, had originally been constructed for Daniel Boone's granddaughter. The rest of the house had been built around the cabin and its old square-cut logs framed the one room that Meg hadn't the heart to put her feminine stamp on when we'd married a few years ago. Oh, I had no complaints. She didn't go crazy putting up lace, or country ducks, or ringlets, or flounces, or whatever you call that girly stuff that pervades home shopping networks, but one could certainly tell a difference in the decor since she'd moved in, and in a good way. Not only did her decorating skills suit my taste exactly, but on one memorable Christmas she'd even given me a full-sized stuffed buffalo. Sure, it was relegated to the den, but a *buffalo!* How could you not love a woman like that? The rest of the house still had plenty of leather furniture, polished wood, some great art, books—all stuff that made you happy to come home. The house, the *cabin*, as we called it, although it was hardly that, was now no longer a work-in-progress. Meg had spent a pretty penny on it since we'd been married, but we could afford it.

Oh, yes, we could afford it.

I'd made a whole bunch of money with an invention I sold to the phone company in the 1990s. I sat on the cash for a while, then let Meg invest it for me. This was before we were married, and Meg Farthing was quite the savvy broker. By the time we'd gotten around to getting hitched, she'd parlayed my small fortune into quite a large one. I didn't *have* to work. I *liked* to work and I enjoyed both of my jobs, police chief and organist. Meg kept her professional hand in as well, although now only for a few select clients. She was also finishing up her term as the Senior Warden of St. Barnabas, a post she was more than happy to relinquish.

A particularly unappetizing chord sounded from the piano. "It's something that Cynthia gave me," I said, struggling to transpose the clarinet part in my head, while keeping the twin bassoons going in the left hand and whistling the occasional flute interlude down an octave. "A Christmas piece. She found it in the basement of the courthouse."

"Sounds awful," said Meg, never one to mince words.

"It's not that bad," I said. "It doesn't help that I only have ten fingers and that this clarinet part is in A." I whistled a few more flute notes.

"How about a beer?" Meg said. "Your holiday beer shipment came today."

I stopped playing. "All of it?"

"I suppose so. There's quite a variety."

"My *Anderson Valley Winter Solstice*? My *Great Divide Hibernation Ale*?"

"I'll check. Shall I surprise you?" asked Meg.

"Absolutely!"

Megan Farthing Konig is a dark-haired beauty of singular loveliness and charm. She's a few years younger than I am and was married once before, just after college. The union didn't last. We'd met, a couple of decades later, on the afternoon she tore through St. Germaine in her late-model Lexus doing about sixty miles an hour. A few hours after I'd pulled her over, we discovered two important things: 1) we were quite compatible, and 2) I could be bribed into not issuing a ticket. We spent the evening listening to music and eating knockwurst and sauerkraut. That she'd listen to a Bach cantata all the way through was the first thing I liked about her. That she liked knockwurst and sauerkraut was the second. After that I lost track.

Following a long courtship, and several proposals, Meg had finally decided that I was marriage material. That was three years ago, and we've never looked back. It was a memorable anniversary. We'd been married on the very night St. Barnabas Church had burned to the ground.

"Here's some refreshment," said Meg, putting a mug down on a table next to the piano. "Maybe this will help with all the wrong notes. Something called *Samuel Smith's Winter Welcome.*"

"I'd forgotten about that one. And these are not wrong notes."

"Are you sure?"

"Yep. The beginning of this piece is in a style that was very hip in the late '20s and early 1930s. Hip, but pretty painful to listen to."

"How so?" asked Meg, sitting down on the piano bench beside me.

"Well, this school reflected the prevailing 'modernist' attitude among intellectuals: that they were a small vanguard leading the way for the masses. The rest of us would only come to appreciate their efforts over time."

"Really? How presumptuous! Speaking as one of the 'Great Unwashed,' I think I'm offended."

"As well you should be. According to their philosophy, music and the other arts need be accessible only to a select cadre of the enlightened. Everyone else would be doomed to listen to jazz or something equally pedestrian."

"Are we finished with that particular artistic view yet?" asked Meg.

"Not by a long shot," I said with a chuckle. I played a few bars at the beginning of the piece. "You know, although Elle de Fournier starts the cantata in this avant-garde style, within a few pages, she begins to break out of it. Almost as if she's turning her back on the sophisticated artistic scene she's spent years becoming part of, and deciding to reach instead for her roots. Listen to how this melody begins to develop."

I played the oboe line over top of a cluster of early 20th century polychords. Then slowly, over the next sixteen measures, the cacophony began to relax as the melody seemed to coerce the accompanying dissonance into submission. Not totally, mind you. Each instrument had its own agenda and the discord would swell occasionally, but the melody wouldn't relent. It pushed its way back into prominence and the other voices had to give way.

"I know that tune," said Meg. "It's a hymn, isn't it?"

"It is," I said. "And listen to what it does."

I continued playing and the hymn turned on itself, weaving in and out amongst the voices, first here, then there. It wasn't a well-known Christmas hymn, but rather an old melody that had flavors of its Scotch-Irish heritage. A haunting, modal tune that may or may not have originated in the Appalachians, but that had certainly been embraced by them, echoing from their crags and hollows as it was sung by generations of mountain folk.

"I'm not convinced," said Meg. "It's not pretty. Christmas music needs to be pretty. Chestnuts roasting and snow falling and angels and *Ave Maria* and *O Magnum Mysterium*. Stuff like that."

"We need to do something different this year. *I* need something different."

"You're just in a bad mood. Crabby," said Meg, decidedly. "Like everyone else in town. Just today, I was having lunch at the Ginger Cat and when I asked politely for some *Pesto alla genovese*, Annie barked that there wasn't any, and why didn't I try to get some down at the Slab since I liked eating there so much."

"The Slab doesn't serve pesto, my pet," I said absently, continuing to concentrate on one of the bassoon parts which had inexplicably just changed clefs.

"Yes, *darling*. That's the point! Are you even listening?"

"Hey," I said, stopping in the middle of what sounded like a D-flat "demolished" chord and looking up at her. "Don't point your Christmas crabbiness at me. I don't even think I would like *Pesto alla* whatever."

Her eyes narrowed. "Oh, you'd like it," she said through clenched teeth. "You'd like it *a lot!*"

"I don't think I *would*," I growled back. "In fact, you could wrap it in bacon, deep fry it in hog fat, and top it with a pork chop, and I wouldn't even taste it!"

Meg laughed, a low, wonderful laugh that I loved to hear. "I'll take that as an apology for your inattentiveness," she said with a giggle. "How about if I put some John Rutter carols on the stereo to cheer us up?"

I grunted at her. "Bah," I said. "Humbug!"

Meg tapped at the music on the piano. "Well, Mr. Grumpy, if you like this thing, why not do it with the choir? If you're right, maybe it will improve everyone's mood. Lord knows, we don't have anything else to work on. You haven't given us anything but a couple of extra-gloomy Advent anthems."

"Maybe I will," I said. "And those anthems aren't gloomy. They're contemplative."

"Oh, I see," said Meg. "Contemplative, eh? Pensive, perhaps? Meant to remind us of our mortality as we repent and prepare for the Glory of Christmas?"

"Exactly," I said. "Advent classics."

"Nonsense. They're gloomy. Gloomy and forlorn."

I could see her point. "Well," I agreed, "perhaps my choices in choir anthems have been a bit ... wintry."

"Wintry, indeed," said Meg. "Whatever you decide to do, you'd better hustle. We only have three more rehearsals before Christmas Eve."

The cold spell hadn't broken, but by ten o'clock on Wednesday the temperature had climbed to a balmy twelve degrees. The sun was bright, almost too bright, and there still hadn't been any snow despite the frigid air mass that had settled over our end of the state. Ten o'clock on a December morning usually found the Slab Café packed. This morning, not. The only customers in the restaurant were Nancy, Dave, Meg, and myself. That is, if you didn't count Cynthia, who might be counted since she wasn't actually "on" this morning, but had just come in for a cup of coffee.

"Cynthia doesn't count," said Pete, gloomily. "She won't be paying for her coffee. So, including you four, that makes five customers this morning."

"We're not paying, either," said Nancy. "We get comped, remember?" She pointed at her badge. "To protect and serve?"

It had been Pete's practice to comp the PD's breakfast tabs at the Slab since he'd first been elected mayor some twenty years ago. In actuality, he'd managed to route some city expenditure money into his café coffers under the guise of mayoral/police departmental breakfast meetings. Unfortunately, once he'd been dethroned, we law enforcement officials still expected the courtesy of a complimentary breakfast. If Pete had needed the money, I might have felt sorry for him.

Pete sighed heavily. "Well, then, if I count Meg, who is *not* a mooching member of our city's finest ..."

"I'm not," Meg assured him.

"That brings the grand total to two. Subtract the three free breakfasts I have to rustle up and I'm one in the hole. Usually by this time on a Wednesday in December, I've done $800 worth of business. I haven't done $800 in the last week."

"Things will pick up," Meg said, in as cheerful a tone as she could muster. "Why, even Hayden is in a better mood."

I nodded and sipped my coffee. "It's true. I am. And the weather is supposed to warm up a bit tomorrow."

"Clear up into the mid-twenties," Dave added. "It'll be like a heat wave."

Pauli Girl McCollough came out of the kitchen carrying a platter of country ham biscuits. "Here y'all are," she said, setting our meal in the center of the table. "This is some first-rate country ham. The biscuits just came out of the oven."

Pauli Girl was in her first semester of nursing school and home for her Christmas break. She was Ardine McCollough's middle child and the only girl. Her older brother, Bud, was known throughout the county for his wine expertise and was attending college at Davidson. I hadn't seen him since Thanksgiving, but I suspected he was close to finishing his fall semester. Pauli Girl's younger brother, Moose-head (Moosey for short), was still in elementary school and his school's Christmas break was still a couple of weeks away.

All three of the McCollough kids had been named by their father, PeeDee McCollough, who was, by all accounts, not a nice person. Not only did he name all three of his children for beer, he was not hesitant in disciplining them, or their mother either, using whatever was handy, be it a belt, a walking stick, or a car antenna. It was when he brought home a piece of airline cable he'd found at the dump that Ardine decided that she and the children might be better off without him.

These kind of "homemade divorces" occasionally happened in the hollers and when PeeDee McCollough disappeared no one looked very hard. No one except for a certain Miss Charity Porkington, the leader of the unmarried women's Sunday School class at the Baptist church where PeeDee had been a regular attendee and deacon. After several weeks of futile calling, Miss Porkington drove up to Ardine's single-wide trailer and asked her, pointblank, what had happened to PeeDee, then fell weeping on the front stoop until Ardine went back into the trailer and came out with her shotgun. It was then that Miss Porkington saw the wisdom of relocating to another county.

"How about some scrambled eggs with this?" asked Dave, taking two ham biscuits and reaching for the strawberry preserves.

"No eggs," snarled Pete. "You'll get what you get." His voice dropped to a mumble. "... Bunch of fat-cat, freeloading city employees ..."

"Why the change in your yearly holiday curmudgeonry?" Cynthia asked me. "Pete's been acting like this for a week now."

"Oh, I'm still embracing my inner Scrooge," I said, "but it sort of has to do with that music you gave me."

"Really?" said Cynthia. "So it's good?"

"It *is* good," I said, at the same time watching Meg catch Nancy's eye and soundlessly move her lips to form the words "No, it's not."

"Quite frankly," I continued, "I'm intrigued. If it was performed on Christmas Eve at St. Barnabas in 1942, someone must remember it."

"So it's the mystery that woos you," said Nancy. It was a statement rather than a question.

"Perhaps," I said, "but it's an attractive and interesting work by a pretty good composer. If the choir can learn it, we can go ahead and perform it on Christmas Eve."

"No, we can't," mouthed Meg.

Chapter 4

Moving to Henry's hometown in the mountains was not something that she wanted to do. At least not yet. But he'd asked her to do it, to be his link to his parents to whom he was not particularly close. He felt guilty about that, and she agreed to move into his small house in St. Germaine. She did not know his parents well, but they were pleasant enough to her, seeing as she was the "right" sort of person and her family was well-connected to the Vanderbilts.

She wrote to Henry everyday—sometimes twice—then sealed her missives inside a special armed forces envelope, addressed it carefully, walked the three blocks to the post office, and mailed it. She didn't know if he got them in a timely fashion, but suspected that he didn't. She didn't receive a letter every day, but then, didn't expect one. His letters to her came in packets. Maybe five, maybe twenty. There was no rhyme nor reason. She might receive a packet of letters on a Tuesday, then nothing for two weeks, then another packet on a Friday, then yet another the following Monday, and Monday's letters were actually written before the letters in the two earlier packets.

She tore through them as quickly as she received them, devouring Henry's words as soon as they landed in her hands, then spent hours putting them in sequence and re-reading them, trying to get a sense of chronology, but not only that. She wanted to, needed to, discern his mood, his level of anxiety, his sentiments about the war. But he only wrote about the weather, about army buddies, about North Africa and the cities he'd seen. He never mentioned the battles he fought, the horrific death she knew he must be witnessing, the inhumanity that was part of his everyday life. She understood that he didn't want to worry her, but this did not assuage her fretfulness.

What she loved the most, and so read over and over, was when he wrote about their coming life together. He had plans, big plans. After he got back to the States, he'd work for the family for a few years to save money, then move into banking when the time was right. Henry Greenaway was going to open a bank. He had the connections from his Yale days and he already had investors. And he wanted her to follow her music career wherever her talent might take her. Children? Sure, but there was no rush. This was his dream—their dream—and he wrote about it often.

"Just what is this?" asked Marjorie suspiciously, thumbing through her copy of *La Chanson d'Adoration*. "Who is this Elle de Fournier? Some friend of yours?"

Marjorie Plimpton was generally the first person to show up for choir rehearsal. She had been a soprano in her youth, but by middle age, cigar smoking and gin consumption had taken her voice down to alto, and now, as she approached her eighties, deep into the tenor section. She swore that if she lived long enough, she'd become a bass even though she didn't much care for reading the bass clef. "I can do it," she said. "It just takes me a little while to count all those lecher lines."

"I don't know anything about Elle de Fournier," I said, "but we'll do some checking."

"Looks hard," said Marjorie, flipping the pages. "And it's all handwritten. This isn't one of them modern sounding thingys, is it? That stuff makes my back hurt."

"Maybe just a little," I admitted.

"Well then, lemme fill up," said Marjorie, getting up from her chair. She retrieved a small silver flask—a flask that had found a permanent home in the hymnal rack of her choir chair—and disappeared behind one of the organ pipe cases.

The choir loft in St. Barnabas Episcopal Church is located in the back balcony. When the terrible Thanksgiving fire destroyed our church building, we chose to model our new structure on the 1904 church, or as close to the original as we could. The choir, therefore, as well as the pipe organ, were relegated to the back balcony. Our architect and contractors added upgrades, as might be expected in a new structure—wireless internet, state-of-the-art sound and recording system, hidden sprinklers—but, on the whole the similarity between the new church and the one that burned was amazing. If a person had visited the church five years earlier, and not been back again until last Sunday, he or she might not have noticed any difference. I held out a hope, though, that whoever it was would notice the new pipe organ. It was a beauty.

The new organ had been designed and constructed by the Baum-Boltoph Organ Company right here in North Carolina. It consisted of forty-three ranks of pipes, thirty-four stops, and was perfect for the space: a long nave, two transepts (side alcoves that formed the "arms" of the traditional cross-shaped building), and enough pews to accommodate our two hundred fifty regular worshippers with room to squeeze in a hundred more for special services. The choir loft could seat thirty singers comfortably and the organ console sat next to the balcony rail, stage left and facing center, from which I played, directed, and kept a watchful eye on both the choir and the people down in the chancel where the altar was located.

The eight-foot-tall stained glass window at the back of the loft depicts a larger-than-life St. Barnabas as a mature apostle. His head is bald on top, and what hair remains above his ears is white. His beard is long and curly and he has a rolled scroll in one hand and a quill clasped to his bosom in the other. He wears his scarlet bishop's robes with a white and gold cope (since he was, after all, the first bishop of Milan), but eschews the mitre, and looks very much like a Roman senator, sandals and all. This is a nineteenth-century depiction that has very little to do with what Barnabas might have looked like, but it *is* an accurate copy of the old stained glass window that had been destroyed in the fire. The inscription reads "St. Barnabas, Son of Encouragement (Acts 4:36)." Barnabas is also known as the "Son of Consolation," but we choose to dwell on the more "uplifting" aspect of our name saint. Occasionally one of the children will sneak up into the choir loft and color St. Barnabas' toenails red using a crayon that has been thoughtfully provided for them in their worship bag. This drives Marjorie crazy and when it happens she spends most of the sermon scrubbing St. Barnabas' toes with her gin-soaked handkerchief trying to make the aggrieved saint presentable.

Michael Baum, the organ builder, had thoughtfully provided me with a secret drawer in the organ bench where I hid my Glock 9. In the old days I kept it handy for the choir rats that were always chewing on the wires. Now, since we had a brand-new, apparently rodent-proof church, I kept it for the tenors.

Bev Greene, Georgia Wester, and Meg came up the stairs and into the loft, one behind the other.

"Well," announced Georgia, "the sopranos are here." Georgia owned Eden Books and generally didn't sing with the choir except during the Advent/Christmas season.

"The good ones are here, anyway," grumbled Bev, just loud enough for me to hear. I assumed that Bev was referring not to all the missing sopranos, but to one in particular: Muffy LeMieux.

Muffy was a soprano whose vocal stylings, as well as her dress, tended toward the Nashvillian. She was determined to become a country star, and her signature look—stretch pants, cowboy boots, and tight angora sweaters in various colors—lent credence to her dream. She had dark red hair and pale, flawless skin. At least that's how the men in the choir described it: flawless. The BRAs (back row altos) were less kind, characterizing her complexion as "well-camouflaged." Muffy was always followed, at not quite arm's length, by her husband Varmit. Varmit LeMieux ostensibly sang in the bass section, but everyone knew he was there to keep an eye on Muffy. There was some history there that we weren't privy to, and no one asked.

"I didn't mean Elaine," muttered Bev, obviously feeling a twinge of remorse. Bev Greene was our church administrator and had her hands full, what with our part-time supply priest beginning to give her grief about his wife's insurance benefits and trying to keep tabs on Kimberly Walnut, our Director of Christian Formation. Kimberly Walnut had decided that Advent wasn't really fun for children, and had invited them to sing a Christian version of *Jingle Bells* in church on the Sunday after Thanksgiving during the Children's Moment. Preferring to take advantage of the Walmart

Liturgical Calendar rather than the one we currently used, Kimberly Walnut had lined all the kids across the steps of the chancel, pointed at her Sunday School accompanist, Heather Frampton, and started the song. The first and second graders howled like banshees.

Christ is born, Christ is born, Christ is born today!
He was sent from heav'n above,
to take your sins away ... HEY!
Angels sing, church bells ring,
children laughing, too.
Celebrate the greatest gift,
from God straight down to you!

I noticed that the children especially enjoyed the *HEY!* part, emphasizing the word with "jazz hands" just as they'd been taught.

"Kimberly Walnut didn't say anything about this during the worship meeting," Bev growled, seated right behind me in the soprano section. "I asked her specifically what she was going to do at the Children's Moment. For heaven's sake! It's not even the first Sunday of Advent yet."

"I wouldn't know," I said. "As you remember, I skipped that meeting."

"Yes, I *do* remember!"

Kimberly Walnut took the solo verse, holding our state-of-the-art wireless microphone.

Long, long time ago, while we were still in sin,
God, He had a plan, to get His people in.
He sent a baby boy, and Jesus was His name.
And all that choose to welcome Him
Will never be the same! ... OH!

"Christ is born, Christ is born, Christ is born today!" the children screamed over the piano.

"*Oy veh!*" said Bev, her head dropping into her hands.

"Take solace in the fact that you may be able to use this against her," I said. "Maybe."

The kids finished to polite applause and raced, pell-mell, back down the center aisle and out the back door to Children's Church. They'd be back for communion.

"I can't fire her," said Bev. "You know what the vestry said. No changes in staff until we get a full-time priest. And now she's gaining support. Not with the parents so much. Mostly with the little old ladies."

"Well, you have to admit there are a whole lot more kids in Sunday School since she took over."

Bev nodded glumly. "Yeah. But I don't know if it's because of her or in spite of her. If she'd just check with me once in awhile ..."

Meg followed Georgia and Bev across the loft to the soprano section, picked up her copy of the cantata, and sat down. "So," she said, "you decided to do it."

"Yep. It's Sydney or the bush."

"Huh?" said Georgia.

"You know ... Sydney or the bush. Hollywood or bust. Banjo or the buzzard."

"I never understand a word you're saying," said Marjorie, reappearing from behind the pipe case with her flask.

"Never mind," I said. "We're doing it."

"Doing what?" asked Rebecca, coming in the stairwell door. She was followed in quick succession by Tiff St. James (my unpaid music intern from Appalachian State) and Elaine Hixon, another soprano. Rebecca and Tiff were altos.

"This cantata," I answered. "*La Chanson d'Adoration.* Christmas Eve. It's on your chairs."

"Huh," said Elaine, picking up the score by the edges and shaking it as if she were trying to extricate spiders from the pages. "I don't mean to sound crabby, but ..."

"No more crabbiness," said Meg. "I proclaim a moratorium on griping."

"Can she do that?" asked Mark Wells. The basses had come into the loft as well, and now there was a steady stream of choristers representing all the sections. We had twenty-two singers on the unofficial choir roster. I was hoping for twenty at rehearsal. I'd be happy with sixteen.

"Yes," I said. "I'm sure it's in our choir constitution, or bylaws, or whatever. The president may declare a moratorium on whatever she chooses."

"Yeah," said Rebecca, "but we don't *have* a president."

"I'd declare a moratorium on *this*," grumped Elaine, still holding the score at arm's length. "I don't like the way it feels. And look at how long the dang thing is. It must be a hundred pages."

"The number of pages is deceiving," I said. "You see, I didn't extract the vocal parts so we all have full scores ..."

"I nominate Meg for choir president," crowed Marjorie. "All in favor?"

"No ... wait ..." said Meg.

"Aye," came the resounding cry.

"Opposed?" asked Meg hopefully.

No answer.

43

"Oh, that's just *great!*" she said.

"Okay, Madame President," said Elaine. "First order of business. If Hayden's gonna make us sing this thing, let's talk about the Christmas party."

"Later," I said. "We have to rehearse. Pull out the anthem for Sunday. *Veni, Veni Emmanuel* by Zoltán Kodály."

"Zoltán?" said Fred May. "His name is Zoltán?" The rest of the basses—Bob Solomon, Phil Camp, and Steve DeMoss—had taken their seats in the back row. In front of them were the tenors: Marjorie, Randy Hatteberg, and Bert Coley. Bert was the best singer, having been in the Appalachian State Concert Choir when he was a student. Now he was a police officer in Boone, but still came and sang when he wasn't on duty. Randy was good. Marjorie was earnest.

In addition to Tiff St. James, the altos in attendance included Martha Hatteberg (Randy's wife), Rebecca, Tiff, and Sheila DeMoss. All were good singers and good sight-readers.

"Zoltán Kodály," I said. "Very famous Hungarian composer and pedagogue. You might remember him from music education. The Kodály Method?"

"Oh, sure," said Tiff. "I didn't know he wrote choral music, though."

"Hey, Tiff," said Fred, "where's Ian?"

"I'm sure I don't know," said Tiff, her color rising slightly.

As if on cue, Dr. Ian Burch, PhD, came through the stairwell door, looked around the choir and made a beeline for the empty chair next to Tiff. Ian was a countertenor, a fine one actually, and had been supplementing our alto section since he'd become infatuated with Tiff St. James just before Halloween. Now, six weeks later, he was still on the prowl. Unfortunately for Dr. Ian Burch, PhD, Tiff was not interested. This wasn't surprising, really. Ian was

44

twice Tiff's age and possibly one of the most unfortunate-looking men in St. Germaine. It wasn't his protruding ears, his small, flat head, or his long, slightly red nose that made him so homely, but rather the cumulative effect of the whole. His dating persona wasn't helped by a rather irritating personality stemming (in Meg's opinion) from a PhD in musicology, a fascination with the unknown music of Guillaume Dufay (1397-1474), and the fashion sense God gave a badger. "For heaven's sake," Meg said. "He wears a cape! A fur-lined cape!"

"Good evening, Tiff," Ian said, sidling his choir chair three inches closer to Tiff's.

"Hi," muttered Tiff.

"Hey," said Marjorie, interrupting any further exchange. "This anthem is in Latin. I don't sing in Latin."

"Sure you do," said Bob from the bass section. "Think back. The *Little Organ Mass? O Vos Omnes? Ave Maris Stella*?"

"Oh, you guys sang in Latin," said Marjorie, "but I was just making words up. If God had wanted us to sing in Latin, he wouldn't have given us uvulas."

Meg and I drove back to the house listening to John Rutter carols, a CD that had magically appeared in her car stereo. If we'd been in my old Chevy pickup, we'd be listening to my Leon Redbone *Christmas Island* album, since Meg had banned it from the house for the duration of the holidays. I'd left my truck parked in front of the police station. I would hitch a ride with Meg back into town tomorrow morning in her Lexus. The heated leather seats made a big difference. The only thing that was heated in the '62 pickup was the exhaust pipe.

"You fixed supper?" Meg asked. "I haven't been home since I left this morning and I'm starved."

"Yes. Yes, I did."

"Well?" she asked.

"Hasenpfeffer," I said. "I got the recipe from Anka Hoffman at the Heidelberg Haus when I was there last week. Delicious! She gave me a couple of rabbits, too. They've been in the freezer."

"Rabbits?" said Meg, the color draining from her face. "I thought those things in the freezer were for Archimedes."

Archimedes was a barn owl that shared our home, but was definitely not what you'd call "tame." He came and went as he pleased, thanks to an electronic window in the kitchen, but spent much of the winter settled either on the head of the stuffed buffalo or on a perch that I'd fashioned above the fireplace in the living room. I supplemented his diet during the cold months either with baby squirrels or chipmunks that I got from my friend Kent Murphee, the medical examiner in Boone. In the summer I switched Archimedes' complementary comestibles to mice. No sense in spoiling him too much. Besides, he could always eat bats and feast on the fledglings in August.

"Well, they were hares, actually. Hasenpfeffer is sort of a stew. Very tasty. I left it simmering, so if Baxter hasn't climbed onto the stove, removed the lid, and eaten the whole thing, it should be ready when we get home." Baxter was a large dog, but not prone to climbing on stoves. I figured we were safe on that count.

"*Hasenpfeffer?*" said Meg again. "*Really?*"

"You'll love it," I said. "Just don't ask what's in it."

"Well, thanks a lot. Now I have to know."

"Hmm. Well, there's the rabbit. Onions, a lot of pepper." I thought for a moment. "Garlic, lemon, thyme, rosemary ... a bunch of spices like that. Oh, yeah. Juniper berries and cloves. And wine. A whole bottle."

"I've never had rabbit, but that doesn't sound too bad. Anything else?"

"I can't remember," I lied, choosing not to tell Meg about the part of the recipe that included braising the pieces of meat in a marinade thickened with the poor bunny's blood. Instead, I changed the subject.

"I thought the cantata went okay considering that it was our first time through it."

"You're dreaming," said Meg. "It's hard to read. It's hard to sing. The harmonies make no sense."

"They *do,* though," I argued. "They just don't go where you want them to. It is different—I'll give you that much. I *will* admit that the hand-written manuscript is not what we're used to. It may take a little time."

Meg just shook her head. "Two weeks left. I hope you know what you're doing. Hey! I just thought of something: 'Waiter, there's a hare in my stew!'"

"Yuk, yuk. Wasn't funny when I tried it on the waitress at the Heidelberg Haus, either."

"Joy to the world," warbled the stereo, "the Lord is come!"

Chapter 5

The Great Christmas Tree Debate at St. Barnabas had raged for almost fifty years. In 1957, Mrs. Frances Kipps Spenser, a fashion coordinator at Herman's Department Store in Danville, Virginia, thought that the usual brightly-colored Christmas ornaments were just not appropriate for a setting of worship, and so began researching and looking for something that would better reflect the Christian faith. What she came up with were Christian symbols made of Styrofoam, gold plastic beads and pearls. The Protestant community immediately clutched these Styrofoam ornaments (but gently ... oh, so gently) to their collective bosoms so fervently that Mrs. Spenser decided to trademark the term Chrismon™—a combination of the words "Christ" and "monogram"—lest some unscrupulous entrepreneur do it later and try to make a buck. She then deeded the trademark to the local Lutheran church, henceforth and forever more to be known as Chrismon Central. There are now rules about how to hang the Chrismons, rules governing acceptable symbols, special gloves required, and so on.

In the 1970s, St. Barnabas got on board the Chrismon train and the Daughters of the King chapter spent one summer working their fingers to the bone making the Chrismons that would be used diligently for the next fifty years. There are only two or three of those Daughters left in the congregation, but they wield considerable influence, and so the specter of the Chrismon tree looms large every Advent.

In direct opposition to the Chrismonites are those who favor the Jesse tree. The Jesse tree has considerably fewer rules than the Chrismon tree and can be decorated in a variety of ways. The Jessetonians of St. Barnabas—mainly a younger crowd—prefer the "natural" look: bird's nests, fruit, stuffed wrens and robins, pine cones, nuts, garlands, and the like. Once, a few years ago, someone snuck a six-foot-long rubber black snake into the branches to represent the serpent in the Garden of Eden. It was quickly removed once Thelma Wingler discovered it. Thelma, then in her seventies, had dropped in early on a Sunday morning and come face to face with the rubber creature while trying to sneak a Chrismon onto the Jesse tree. It was Father Tony who found her sitting next to the tree, her eyes wide and unblinking, a crushed Styrofoam Jesus fish in her twitching hand. Tony had been in the sacristy and heard the wavering scream. The ambulance came and picked her up, and Thelma spent the rest of Advent in an assisted living facility, trying to get the dosage of her nerve pills adjusted and shrieking at black extension cords.

The problem with all of this is that we can't actually have a "Christmas tree" at St. Barnabas. The rules are simple. No vestiges of Christmas before Christmas, and Christmas is legally December 25th at 12:00 AM. We hedge on Christmas Eve and pretend that the five o'clock service is really a Christmas service, but that's as close as we'll come to breaking through the invisible Christmas wall.

Since we can't have a Christmas tree, a Chrismon tree or a Jesse tree will suffice. Throw a few stuffed birds or a Styrofoam Chi Rho up in the branches and no one seems to know the difference. The vestry finally came to a compromise several years ago, deciding to placate both theological factions by alternating the trees each year. This is the year of the Chrismons, and it may be their last. For the past decade or so, Wendy Bolling has kept the decorations in a large box in her basement, but over the summer a family of possums got in and made a mess of a lot of the decorations. Possums aren't known for eating Styrofoam, but these critters certainly gave it their best shot. Wendy had tried to do some repair work with a hot-glue gun, straight pins, and a whole lot of glitter, but it was clear that if the Chrismonites were to hold their sway, there would have to be some new ornaments constructed. I didn't see it happening. In my opinion, the days of unemployed ladies of a certain age sitting down together and doing crafts have passed.

The same rules that govern church holiday decorations also govern the singing of Christmas carols and hymns. No *Hark the Herald Angels* or *While Shepherds Watched Their Flocks* before Christmas. Sure, I hedge a bit and throw in *Lo, How A Rose E'er Blooming* and *In the Bleak Midwinter*, but I justify them with the scriptures appointed for the day. If we're talking full-blown Christmas hymns —angels and shepherds and mangers and such—it just isn't happening. Meg hates this, as does most of the choir, and to tell the truth, I'm not really much of a fan either. Don't get me wrong. I love the twelve days of Christmas as much as the next guy and I'm a big fan of the Liturgical Police, but who really wants to sing *Joy to the World* in January?

Unfortunately, on this Sunday—the second Sunday of Advent—there was no getting away from the prophetic, foreboding air of the lectionary. The Book of Malachi: *But who can endure the day of his coming, and who can stand when he appears? For he is like a refiner's fire and he will purify the descendants of Levi and refine them like gold and silver, until they present offerings to the LORD in righteousness.* The Gospel according to Luke: *The word of God came to John son of Zechariah in the wilderness. He went into all the region around the Jordan, proclaiming a baptism of repentance for the forgiveness of sins.*

Those people who wanted to sing *The First Nowell* were just plain out of luck. Our anthem by Kodály was fine and the tune (*O Come, O Come, Emmanuel*) was at least familiar and might even be considered "Christmasy" by some. The hymns, however, lacked a certain festive air. It was my fault. I'd picked them back in the fall, not realizing what a blue funk the whole town would be in come December.

Our interim priest didn't help matters any. Father Howard "Ward" Shavers was newly retired and had come up to the mountains from South Florida. Father Shavers and his wife Gina were more in tune with a "contemporary" service than the traditional worship of St. Barnabas. It wasn't that he came in and tried to save us from ourselves as many priests did, but rather that he just got lost in the service, had a hard time with the prayer book, didn't know any of the Advent hymns in the hymnal, and really wondered why *The First Nowell* wasn't an option.

And crabbiness was still in full force.

"Ian," I said as soon as the Sunday service was over, "I wonder if you might lend your expertise in the musicological department. I need someone to do a little research."

In addition to Dr. Ian Burch's talent in the countertenor department, he had put his terminal degree in music history to some practical use as well. Dr. Burch owned and operated the Appalachian Music Shoppe in downtown St. Germaine. The shop was a small store that specialized in reproductions of Medieval and Renaissance instruments: crumhorns, sackbuts, rauschpfeifes, hurdy-gurdies, and the like. He didn't have a big walk-in business, but he did brisk internet sales to schools, madrigal groups, and other parties that found the *wurstfaggot* (or sausage-bassoon) somehow irresistible.

Ian's small, dark eyes lit up and he smiled at me through uneven teeth. "Happy to help. Of course you realize that my specialty is the composers of the Burgundian School."

"Yeah," I said. "Not that. I need you to find out about Elle de Fournier. Her style seems to be rooted in the modernist movement active in Paris in the '20s and '30s. I couldn't find her online, but she's an accomplished composer. There must be something about her somewhere."

Ian looked thoughtful for a moment. "I have some people I can call," he said. "Obviously, I have bibliographic sources that you can only guess at. I'll find out."

"That'd be great, Ian. Thanks."

Chapter 6

On Monday morning, I found Mattie Lou Entriken, Wynette Winslow, and Marjorie in the kitchen of the church, diligently making sandwiches to take to the Salvation Army kitchen in Boone. This was something that they did every Thursday afternoon without fail. If they were here on a Monday, something was up.

"Just came in for a cup of coffee," I said, waving my empty mug. "What are you lovely ladies doing here?" I walked over to the Bunn coffee machine and poured myself a cup of Community Dark Roast, the church's coffee of choice.

"The Salvation Army called this morning," said Wynette. "They're running out of food every day now."

"It's the cold weather," said Mattie Lou. "Lord knows, I hate making these sandwiches, but it's Christmastime."

I gestured toward Marjorie with my coffee cup. "What are you doing here, Marjorie? As I recall, you're having an all-out skirmish with the Salvation Army."

"That was last year," said Marjorie, not the least bit defensive. "It's just that they wouldn't let me ring the little bell."

"That wasn't the Salvation Army, dear," said Wynette, spreading some pimento cheese on a piece of white bread. "That was those nudists over at Camp Possumtickle. They were collecting for their *Toys for Nekkid Children* drive or some such thing. They didn't even *have* a bell. Just a red plastic bucket."

"Huh?" said Marjorie. "Really? You sure? I thought they were Salvation Army. They had clothes on. And Santa hats. One of 'em had a tambourine."

"Pretty sure," said Wynette. "And you *have* to wear clothes outside the Kmart. It's a state law."

"Yep," agreed Mattie Lou. "State law. I read it in the paper."

"Well, dang!" said Marjorie. "I didn't know they were nudists."

"I'm sure it was all for a good cause," I said. "While I have all you ladies here, I have some questions I'd like to ask you."

"Are you gonna interrogate us?" asked Mattie Lou. "Do I need my lawyer?"

I laughed. "This is not an official inquiry. I'm just looking for information."

"Okay, then," said Wynette. "Shoot." She put down her spreading knife and wiped her hands on her apron.

"Yeah, shoot," added Marjorie.

Wynette Winslow and Mattie Lou Entriken, both now in their late seventies, had been friends since childhood, and had been members of the church since they were born. They were the two saintly matriarchs of St. Barnabas. As far as they were concerned, Marjorie Plimpton was a Johnny-come-lately, having joined the church when she was seventeen and only being a member for sixty-two years.

"Okay," I said. "What do you remember about Christmas Eve, 1942?"

"What?" said Wynette. "1942? I can't remember what I had for lunch last Tuesday!"

Marjorie gave a cackle.

"I remember that year very well," said Mattie Lou, her smile fading. "I remember because I had to spend the whole school year and the next with my grandparents in Raleigh. Papa was sent home from the Navy because he had tuberculosis. Momma took him to New Mexico to get better. I was just fourteen." Her voice dropped. "He died anyway. July 22, 1943."

"I'm sorry, dear," said Wynette, putting a hand on Mattie Lou's shoulder.

Mattie Lou placed her hand on top of Wynette's and gave her a sad smile. "I still think about him."

"Sure you do," said Wynette.

"That was during the war, right?" asked Marjorie.

"It was," I said. "The year after Pearl Harbor. I'm trying to find out about a Christmas piece that was sung here at St. Barnabas on Christmas Eve that year. The world premiere of a cantata."

"I hadn't moved to St. Germaine yet," said Marjorie. "I joined the choir as soon as we moved to town, but that was in 1945. The year after the war."

"I wasn't in the choir," said Wynette, "but my mother was. She wouldn't let me join because she said I had my father's tin ear." She laughed. "I didn't even know what that meant till years later. She was right, though."

"Ah, well," I said. "I thought it might be worth a try. All the bulletins were lost in the fire. You three were my only hope."

"Hang on, now," said Wynette, "I didn't say I didn't remember 1942. I just can't remember last Tuesday. Now that you mention that Christmas cantata, I do recall the hubbub."

"Really?" My hopes went up. "What kind of hubbub?"

"Well," said Wynette, "I was fourteen that year, the same as Mattie Lou." She beetled her brow and looked thoughtful. "It seems to me that there was a big to-do made over the composer. It was a woman, wasn't it?"

"Yes," I said. "A woman named Elle de Fournier."

Wynette shook her head. "I don't remember the name and I don't think I knew her. She might have

55

been a local girl, but if she was, I never heard of her, before or since."

"So, probably not a local," I said, my detective sense tingling. I pulled a pen out of my pocket and jotted the new fact onto a paper napkin that was lying on the counter.

Mattie Lou gave me *the look*. "A napkin? Oh, *really,* detective. Where's your notebook?"

"Don't give me any grief," I said. "I'm collecting clues and formulating hypotheses. There may be more information to be gleaned."

"Probably not," said Wynette. "Anyway, it didn't happen."

"What didn't happen?"

"The Christmas cantata. I remember that part very well. It was Christmas Eve and Mother came home from rehearsal crying. Then she and my father went into the parlor, closed the door, and didn't come out for about an hour. I remember because the Christmas ham burned and I got in trouble for not taking it out of the oven in time. My sister and I had our ears pressed against the parlor door the whole time trying to hear what was going on."

"Did you ever find out why she was crying?"

"They never told us. We just ate our burnt ham, hung up our stockings, and went to bed early. Well, early for Christmas Eve. That was the only time growing up that we skipped the midnight mass at St. Barnabas."

"So," I said, trying to get Wynette's story straight in my head, "the Christmas cantata wasn't performed?"

"Nope," said Wynette. "I don't believe it was. Not that year, anyway."

I looked over at Mattie Lou. She shrugged and went back to spreading pimento cheese across the faces of her half-made sandwiches. "Like I said, I wasn't here."

"Anything else?" I asked Wynette. "Anything at all?"

She shook her head. "That's it. But if I think of anything, I'll give you a call."

"I wonder if those nudies need someone to ring their bell this year?" said Marjorie.

Chapter 7

She'd joined the Episcopal choir the third week she had been in St. Germaine. She'd been invited by Mary Alice Sterling, whom she had met downtown on one cool September afternoon. The choir had made her feel very welcome, much more welcome than her new, extended family, and she made friends very quickly. The choir director, a limpid man named Stan Dearman, had been deliriously happy to have a soprano who could read music, not to mention a choir member in possession of such a clear, bell-like voice. When, in the course of conversation, Mary Alice found out that she was a composer as well, and, in fact, had studied with Nadia Boulanger herself, her friend spilled the beans to Mr. Dearman, even though she'd been sworn to secrecy.

That Mary Alice! What kind of friend would betray such a trust? Yet for all her indignant airs, she was inwardly pleased, and even more pleased when Mr. Dearman asked her if she might have composed anything that they could sing for Christmas.

Why, yes, she'd fibbed. A short cantata actually. It would be a world premiere. Did he think the choir would be up for such an opportunity? She might even get Mademoiselle to send a letter of congratulations to the choir. Mr. Dearman expressed his excitement, but was skeptical. Could she really get a letter from Nadia Boulanger? Could we have the newspaper publish it? Oh, I think so, she replied. Mademoiselle came over to America just before the war started and is currently residing in Massachusetts. I have her address.

And so the deal was sealed.

Now she had to write it.

The painfully frigid temperatures we'd been experiencing in the mountains had abated, and the Slab Café was full. If the Slab was any indication, St. Germaine would be full of shoppers by ten o'clock. Meg had procured a table by the front window and was waiting for me when I came in. The police department had a reserved table in the back, or so we liked to think, but when space ran out, Pete or Noylene, either one, was quick to grab Nancy's "reserved" sign and toss it behind the counter. Paying customers outranked the PD.

"I already ordered for you," said Meg. "Pete wants to turn these tables over and make up for lost revenue."

"Fine with me. I'm in a hurry, anyway." I pulled out a chair and sat down. "What am I having?"

"Well, since Manuel is back in the kitchen, I thought you'd like the special. Cheese Grits Mexicano."

"Sounds great." I waved an empty coffee cup at Noylene. She made a face at me, then pointed at Pauli Girl who took the hint and made her way over to the table, stopping to fill a couple of empty cups *en route*.

"Y'all need some coffee?" she said when she got to our table.

"Absolutely," I said, holding my cup aloft. "How was your semester?"

"Pretty good," Pauli Girl said. "Nursing's hard, but I like it. Right now I'm working on my LPN degree, but I think I might go ahead and become a Registered Nurse."

"That's wonderful," said Meg. "Have you gotten any practical experience?"

Pauli Girl nodded. "When I'm not here, I'm volunteering over at Sunridge Assisted Living. The nurses have me working with an old woman. I'm like her ... well ... helper."

"Her caregiver?" said Meg.

"Yeah, like that." Pauli Girl smiled at her. Pauli Girl McCollough was the prettiest girl in three states. She'd always been beautiful and had been fending off the heartsick boys in Watauga County for several years. She was determined, though, to leave the haunts and hollers where she grew up and she viewed education as her way out. It was a dream that Meg and I were happy to fund, even though Pauli Girl had saved every penny that she made since she started waiting tables when she was fourteen.

"What's her name?" asked Meg.

"Bessie Baker," said Pauli Girl. She lowered her voice to a conspiratorial whisper. "And just between us, she is mean as a *snake!* She used to be a teacher."

"English teacher," said Pete. He walked up to the table and put two orders of Cheese Grits Mexicano on the table. "I'm gonna need a caregiver, too, if this keeps up," he said. "Look there." He pointed toward the door and I saw that, in the five minutes since I had come in, a line had formed at the front of the café and now people were lining up in front of the window and down the block.

"Wow," I said. "The thermometer still hasn't risen above the freezing mark."

"Yeah, but the sun is shining, and Rosa and Cynthia are out there handing out hot chocolate."

"When did Rosa start back?" I asked. Rosa Zumaya was Manuel's wife, a short, plump, middle-aged Mexican woman with a smile as wide as she was.

"Yesterday," Pete said. "Didn't need her last week. We didn't have any customers."

"You have them now," said Meg, "so quit complaining!"

"I'll try to cut back," said Pete with a grin. "I may be getting my Christmas spirit back. I'm feeling sort of ... I don't know ... charitable."

"Hang on," said Pauli Girl. "How'd you know Miss Baker was an English teacher?"

"I had her for English," said Pete. "We all did, back before St. Germaine High School closed and everyone moved to the new county school. She was a monster. 'Baker the Grade Shaker.' That's what we called her. She was tough as a boiled owl."

"She's still tough," admitted Pauli Girl. "And rather difficult."

"I know her," I said, "although I never had her for English. She was on the vestry at St. Barnabas when I was hired twenty years ago and she was ancient then." I took a sip of my coffee. "I believe she was the only dissenting vote."

Meg giggled.

"Then she made my life miserable for about five years. Complaints about the hymns, the anthems, the psalms. The organ was too loud, the service was too long, and why didn't we do Morning Prayer? She had a standing Monday morning appointment with Father Tony just to complain about the previous Sunday. He kept a notebook and gave it to me before he retired. Three hundred pages."

"Only five years?" said Meg. "Why'd she stop?"

I shrugged. "I don't know. Maybe she just wore out. Maybe Father Tony told her to lay off."

"Maybe she decided that you weren't going to get any better," suggested Pete.

"She had a stroke," said Pauli Girl. "In 1992. It was in her chart. She recovered pretty well."

"I've never seen her in church," said Meg. "At least I don't think so. I certainly don't know her."

"Hey," I said. "I just had a thought. If Bessie Baker was living in St. Germaine at the time, maybe she used to sing in the choir. Even if she didn't, she might shed some light on what happened on Christmas Eve in 1942. Wynette didn't know much, but remembered that the cantata was cancelled at the last minute. They may have even cancelled the midnight service."

"Are you talking about that music that Cynthia found?" Pete said.

"Yep," I said. "We're singing it on Christmas Eve. The note Nancy found in the score said that it was premiered at St. Barnabas that Christmas, but now it seems that it never happened. Maybe Bessie Baker knows something." I turned to Pauli Girl. "How old is she?"

"She's in her nineties."

"She might have been what ... late twenties? Early thirties?"

"Probably," agreed Pauli Girl.

"So, she *might* have been in the choir," I said, then had another thought. "How's her memory?"

"Her short term memory isn't good," admitted Pauli Girl, "but you know what? She's good at remembering stuff that happened a long time ago."

"She was a helluva teacher," said Pete. "We hated her when we were in school, but she was one of those teachers that, you know, when you're out in the world, you realize that, wow, you really actually learned something."

"I had a few like that," admitted Meg. "You should send her a card or something and tell her what she meant to you."

"Nah," said Pete. "Too touchy-feely. But you know, a bunch of us from the high school always get together after Christmas. Sort of a reunion. Maybe I'll suggest that a few of the girls go over to see the old bat. That should do it for my seasonal benevolence."

"No, I don't think so," said Meg. "Your seasonal benevolence is just beginning. It's payback time. Remember when I did your taxes last year and saved you a pot-load of money and you said if there was anything I ever wanted ..."

"I do not remember that," said Pete, going pale. "I definitely do *not* remember that."

"I remember it quite well," I said.

"Anyway," said Meg, "I'm the president of the choir, and you and Cynthia are going to come and sing on Christmas Eve. Not only that, you're coming to all the rehearsals and singing on Sunday mornings as well."

Now it was my turn to go pale. I had heard Pete sing. Cynthia was fine, but Pete?

"Wait a minute," I said. "Pete's extremely busy."

"I *am* busy," said Pete. "Anyway, when I said that, I meant that I'd give you a pie or something. I have things to do. Important things. Like ..." he struggled, panic evident in his eyes. "Like, I've got to go visit that old lady in the nursing home."

Pauli Girl laughed out loud and headed for another table, coffee pot at the ready. "Nice try, Pete," she said.

"No way out," said Meg. "You promised. I've already asked Cynthia and she said she's happy to come. Rehearsal is tonight at seven."

"I heard *all y'all* were looking for singers," said a voice from the top of the choir stairs. I looked up from where I was seated on the organ bench and saw Goldi Fawn Birtwhistle filling the doorway.

"We're always glad to welcome new choir members," said Meg. "Are *y'all* a soprano or an alto?" Meg was using the singular *y'all*, as opposed to the collective *all y'all*. *Y'all* is also permissible as a collective pronoun, but once *all y'all* has been introduced into the conversation, it is simply good manners to follow suit.

"I'm a soprano, I guess," said Goldi Fawn, maneuvering her heft past the occupied chairs of the tenor and bass sections. "I like to sing the tune."

"Good luck with that," muttered Muffy. "There ain't no tune that I can find. Not in this thing."

"I usually sing solos," Goldi Fawn said to Muffy. "You know, with an accompaniment track? My signature song is *Christmas Shoes*. It's a song about a little boy who wants to buy some shoes for his dyin' momma at Christmas so she can look pretty when she goes to meet Jesus."

"I sing that song, too," said Muffy. "It's beautiful!" She wiped a single tear from her eye. "But Hayden won't let us sing with a track."

Goldi Fawn Birtwhistle gave her a smile and a wink. "That's okay. I'm singing it at the Lion's Club Christmas luncheon in Boone next week. Wanna come?"

"Yeah!" said Muffy. "You think I could sing something, too?"

"Oh, I'm *sure* you could!" said Goldi Fawn, choosing an empty chair next to her new friend. "I know the program chairman. She comes in every week to get her stars done and her hair colored."

The choir had grown since Sunday, thanks to some heavy-handed recruitment by Meg and Bev. I'd also made a few phone calls and now we numbered twenty-five. Codfish Downs had agreed to sing and was a good, if aging, tenor. Codfish made his living selling fresh mountain trout out of the trunk of his

'98 Pontiac. Most of the trout farmers in the area thought that he made his living by selling *stolen* fresh mountain trout out of his trunk. This accusation had never been proven and until I had some evidence to the contrary, I had to view Codfish's wares as not only legitimately procured, but also very tasty. If he *was* poaching trout, the farmers couldn't figure out how he was doing it. Fresh fish were a seasonal delicacy, however, and when the temperature dropped into the single digits, the trout became much harder to come by. Hence, when I offered Codfish a few bucks to sing with us, he jumped at the chance.

Nancy didn't actually *jump* at the chance, but did agree to join us once Meg asked her nicely. Annie Cooke heard Bev and Elaine talking about the cantata over at the Ginger Cat and was invited to sing when she'd expressed a previously forgotten pleasure in singing Ralph Vaughan William's *Hodie* years ago with her college choir.

Pete and Cynthia, good as their word, were on hand. Pete found a chair in the far back of the choir loft, beside Mark Wells.

A surprise—a *pleasant* surprise—was Rhiza Walker. As Raymond Chandler so aptly put it, Rhiza was a blonde, a blonde to make a bishop kick a hole in a stained glass window. She'd been married to St. Barnabas' Senior Warden once removed. Now she was divorced and her ex, Malcolm Walker, was finishing a seven to ten year plea deal at a minimum security facility. Not hurting for money, she'd been living in Europe for the past few years, but I'd seen her in town on Monday, and so invited her to come and sing. She'd been an undergraduate music major at the University of North Carolina when we'd met. I was in graduate school at the time, and we'd dated for a while. When she graduated, though, she married Malcolm. It was Rhiza, in fact, who told me that Pete was looking for a police chief all those many years ago. I remembered her as a wonderful soprano. I was hoping she still was.

"I have an announcement," said Dr. Ian Burch, PhD, standing up. "I'm having a sale on zinks and lysards at the Music Shoppe," he said. "I've gotten a double shipment by mistake. I also have a selection of handmade snoods just in from Luxembourg."

"Hang on," said Marjorie. "You've got skinks and lizards?"

"Zinks and ly-*zards*," corrected Ian, putting the accent on the final syllable.

"How much?" said Goldi Fawn, obviously never one to pass up a bargain."

"Half price," said Ian.

"Save me one of them skinks, then," said Goldi Fawn. "A green and red one."

Ian looked confused for a moment. "Green and red?" he said.

"Hawk your wares later, Ian," I interrupted. "Did you find out anything about Elle de Fournier?"

"Who's that?" whispered Goldi Fawn to Meg, who was sitting on Goldi Fawn's other side.

"The composer of our cantata," Meg whispered back.

Ian shook his head. "No, I did not, and I'm bound to tell you that if *I* could not find out anything, there is probably nothing to find." He sat down, then stood back up quickly. "Half price on zinks," he said hurriedly, "sixty percent off the lysards. Snoods are full price." Then he sat again.

"Well, choir," I said, "here's what I know. *La Chanson d'Adoration* was written by Elle de Fournier and was to be premiered at St. Barnabas on Christmas Eve, 1942. For some reason—and no one seems to know why, at least no one we've found yet—

the performance was cancelled. The chances are very good that this cantata has *never* been performed."

"So this would be the world premiere then?" asked Randy.

"I expect so," I said.

"Cool," said Tiff. "Can I put this on my resumé?"

"Absolutely, you can!" said Goldi Fawn. "I got all kinds of stuff on my resumé. Like this one time, Wynonna Judd came in to get her stars done ..."

"What a great story!" I said, cutting her short. "So let's start at the beginning and see if we can get a handle on this thing."

An hour and a half later, we'd rehearsed all four movements of the cantata and the entire choir was frazzled. I was frazzled, too. Frazzled but determined.

"How about a break?" I suggested. "We could use one."

"Nah," said Bob Solomon. "I'd rather get this over with. Let's just do it."

The other choir members, noticeably frustrated, nodded.

"Okay," I said. "Then close your books. Time to clear your brains."

The books closed.

"Here's the thing," I said. "This is a difficult piece, but it's not *that* difficult."

"There's no time signature," complained Tiff. "I'm having a tough time counting."

"There are no bar lines," said Georgia. "Just these half lines, and they're different in every part."

"There's no key signature," said Bert. "I don't know where 'tonic' is."

"The words are weird," said Sheila. *"The Song of Solomon?"*

All this was true, of course. The notation was difficult and not what anyone was used to. In addition, it was handwritten and that took some getting used to as well. The text was not the usual Christmas story.

"Listen," I said. *"The Song of Solomon* is sometimes viewed as a messianic text, especially during the time that this music was written. In fact, until the middle of the last century, *The Song* was regarded by theologians as an allegory describing the relationship of Christ and the Church. It's Advent."

"And then there's the whole apple tree/Garden of Eden thing," added Bev. "Okay, I buy it."

"Stand up," I ordered. "Open your scores to the first movement."

The choir complied.

"Relax. Take a deep breath. Close your eyes. Understand that singing is a gift and you are part of that gift. 'Music washes away from the soul the dust of everyday life.' I don't know who said it, but it's true enough."

I looked across the choir. Surprisingly, all their eyes were closed.

"Now, just *listen* to each other. Listen to the music. Lose yourself in it, but *think*. You know the notes. You *know* how to sing this." I paused for a long moment, then said, "Okay, look at me."

I played their opening phrase, then raised my arms from the organ console and conducted the downbeat. Two measures later I quit conducting and my mouth dropped open.

As the apple tree among the trees of the wood,
so is my beloved among the sons.
I sat down under his shadow with great delight,
and his fruit was sweet to my taste.

He brought me to the banqueting house,
and his banner over me was love.

The choir kept singing (and *what* singing!), going through the entire movement, beginning to end, without a break. They finished together, looked at me and I cut them off. The final chord echoed through the church, perfectly in tune, perfectly sung. This had never happened, not once in the twenty-odd years I'd been at St. Barnabas. Not once in *all* my years of conducting. It just hadn't happened. I wasn't sure, until now, that it *could* happen. Not with a volunteer choir, anyway.

Silence filled the church. No one made a sound, not for a solid minute. It was as if everyone was afraid even to take a deep breath. Then Elaine said in a soft voice, "Holy cow!"

"Was that us?" whispered Georgia.

"It was," Meg whispered back.

"Well, I'll be a three-legged horned-toad," said Pete. "Does this happen all the time? I might just join up."

"Let's sing it again," said Randy. "Maybe it was an accident."

The rest of the choir agreed emphatically. I looked around. Each of them, every single one, had a look of wonder on their faces. I gave them their starting notes and they sang it again.

No mistake.

Silence again, then: "We have *got* to rehearse tomorrow night!" said Bert Coley, excitedly. "I have a poker game, but I'll skip it."

"We *have* to," agreed Martha. "No way around it. We still have three movements to learn. We can sing this one on Sunday morning, but we've *got* to have some more rehearsals!"

I was speechless. This was something out of my experience.

"Okay," Meg said decidedly, "a Thursday rehearsal. Who *can't* come?"

"Oh, man!" said Varmit. "Muffy and me got tickets to the monster truck rally in Bristol. Amy Grant is doing the pre-rally concert."

"We've seen Amy before, Varmit," said Muffy. "And Bigfoot ain't even going to be there. He blew a head gasket or something."

"These tickets are nonrefundable!" Varmit argued.

"We'll scalp 'em on the internet," said Muffy with finality. "I can double our money." Varmit knew when he was licked.

"I have a party I'm supposed to be at," said Steve DeMoss.

"Me, too," said Sheila, looking daggers at Steve, "but we're not going."

"I'm not complaining," said Steve. "I didn't want to go anyway."

"Hey!" said Elaine. "That's *my* party!"

"Oops," said Sheila with an apologetic smile. "Sorry. We'll be there when the rehearsal is over."

"The party doesn't start till eight," said Elaine. "It's just a little get-together. So what if I get there an hour or so late? Billy can handle it."

"Wow," said Annie. "That's brave."

"Oh, I owe him," said Elaine. "He did the same thing to me last summer. Invited a bunch of his customers over and then got 'held up' at the shop."

"Let's sing it again," said Marjorie. "There's something strange happening. Singing it ... singing it just makes me feel good."

"It's euphoric," agreed Rebecca.

"Enchanting," said Bev.

70

"It's like how I felt when I first saw the Grand Canyon," said Cynthia, trying to find the words. "I can't even catch my breath. I don't know ..."

"It's like something unbelievably beautiful," said Rhiza, putting her arm around Cynthia and giving her a hug. "You just don't know how to explain it."

"It's like Christmas," said Meg.

Chapter 8

It wasn't as easy as she remembered. When she'd been immersed in the music, when she'd had two and three lessons a week, when she'd been playing piano at the restaurant, composing had come to her as if it were second nature. Now, four years later, she found that writing music was ... difficult. She struggled with themes, she struggled with harmonies, and she couldn't find the voice that she knew was there. She pored over her old compositions and looked for clues, hints on how to tap into her dormant talent. At least she hoped it was only dormant. What if it was gone completely?

She'd been going over Christmas texts, but couldn't find anything that spoke to her. Then, after a month of agonizing, she threw every sketch into the waste bin, sat down at the piano in frustration and placed her hands on the keys. Mozart, she thought. Mozart to clear her mind. It always worked. She began to play.

She wasn't thinking about the cantata at all. She was thinking about Henry, her family, her new church friends, the upcoming holiday, and then she realized what was flowing from her fingers. Not Mozart.

She picked up her pen and started writing.

The next morning, I drove to the station early, and stopped by the Piggly Wiggly to pick up a box of donuts. Amelia Godshaw was the only checkout girl on duty, even though characterizing her as a "girl" was to overstate her status by about sixty years.

Roger Beeson, the manager, was tucked away in his "office," a raised twelve-by-twelve, half-walled cubicle containing a desk, a safe, and a couple of chairs, from which he could survey his domain. Amelia was not known as a "people person," and was most probably packing heat under her checkout counter. It didn't do to irritate Amelia, and Roger might have gotten rid of her except that, for some reason, he couldn't keep any help at the Pig for more than a month or two. Amelia and her friends, Hannah and Grace, were the only employees he could count on not to rob him blind and to show up for their shifts. There was also a stock-boy named Clem, but no one had ever heard him speak.

I was in line at Amelia's checkout counter. In front of me was a woman I didn't know and in front of her was Elaine Hixon. The woman in front of me looked irritated, tapping a bottle of mouthwash angrily on the conveyor belt. Elaine had half a cartful of groceries and was a few items into her checkout routine.

"I'm having a party this evening," Elaine said to Amelia. "A Christmas party."

"Goody for you," grumped Amelia. She rang up a cheese ball from the deli Christmas end-cap, on sale for $3.95.

"Could we hurry it up?" said the next-in-line woman.

"I'm going as fast as I can," said Amelia. "You wanna do it?"

"Amelia," said Elaine, "are you having your hair done at the Beautifery? It just looks lovely."

Amelia blinked, blinked again, and then smiled. "Well, yes, I am," she said. "Noylene's got a new girl. We're trying a reddish blonde with a lemon rinse." She lowered her voice. "She also told me that new opportunities are just around the corner."

"How exciting," Elaine said to Amelia. She spotted me in the back of the line. "Hayden! Good morning!"

"Morning," I said, giving her a wave with my free hand.

"Listen," said the woman, "I've got an appointment in town and I'm already late."

"Who are you meeting?" asked Elaine.

"None of your business!" snapped the woman.

"I only ask," said Elaine, as she pointed to the plate glass windows that comprised the front of the store, "because I think your car slid down the hill and into that ditch."

The woman screamed, dropped her mouthwash, and stared at her car, the front end of which, as Elaine had described, was pointing, headlights down, into the drainage ditch in front of the Piggly Wiggly.

"Oh, my God!" she cried. "How? ... What?..."

"You probably just parked on a patch of ice," said Elaine. "Don't worry. Billy's right around the corner with his Bobcat scraping another parking lot. I'll give him a call." She flipped open her phone, punched a button, and a minute later dropped her phone back into her purse.

"He's on his way. He's got a chain. You'll be out in three shakes."

"How much is this going to cost me?" said the woman, resignation and disgust evident in her voice.

"Why, nothing, dear," said Elaine. "Don't be silly. It's Christmas, after all."

The woman's mouth dropped open. Then, a moment later, she said, "Thank you. Sorry I snapped at you before."

"Oh," said Elaine, waving a hand absently in her direction, "it's nothing."

The woman turned to Amelia. "And I'm sorry I was cross with you." She searched for a compliment.

"You're doing a great job there ... ringing things up. You're the best grocery checker I've seen in a long while, I can tell you."

"Well ..." said Amelia, smiling just a little.

"I'm just on edge," said the woman. "I'm new in town and I'm supposed to meet the president of the library council at eight. Now I'm going to be late. I'm a caterer and I'm trying to get the library patrons' Christmas party job."

"Louise?" said Amelia. "You're meeting Louise Harrison?"

"Why ... yes."

"Pfft," said Amelia. "She's my next door neighbor. We're thick as thieves. Lemme give her a call." Amelia grabbed a phone from under the counter and quickly dialed a number from memory. "Louise? This is Amelia. Yeah ... just fine. You know that caterer you're supposed to meet with?" Amelia put her hand over the mouthpiece and looked at the woman. "Jacki?" she asked. The woman nodded.

"Well, she's just gonna be a tad late. We've had a little accident down at the Pig. No problem? Great!"

The woman beamed.

"And Louise," said Amelia, "you just might as well go on and hire her. She's a real sweet person and she can cook like nobody's business. Yep ... I'll tell her and she'll be there as soon as Billy gets her car out of the ditch."

Amelia clicked the phone off and put it down beside the register.

"No rush," said Amelia with a big smile. "She can't wait to meet you."

"I ... I don't know what to say," said Jacki.

"Oh, here's Billy," said Elaine, looking out the window. The other ladies followed her gaze and saw Billy's mini-dozer making its way across the parking lot toward Jacki's car.

"Did I hear that you're having a party tonight?" Jacki asked Elaine.

"Yes, I am," said Elaine.

"I have some cakes in the back seat that I'm going to show to Mrs. Harrison. But after that, may I drop them by your house for your party? No charge." She put a finger to her lips and looked concerned. "That is, if they're still all right."

"Aren't you sweet," said Elaine, with a big smile. "I'll bet they're just fine. Your car was hardly moving and barely bumped into that ditch."

Jacki nodded. "I hope so."

"Thank you," said Elaine. "Having those cakes would save me a good deal of time and I have a choir rehearsal before the party. Here, let me give you my address."

"Do you have some cards?" asked Amelia. "I can put them here by the register. We always have people asking for caterers. Especially during the holidays."

"You bet!" said Jacki. She dug around in her purse and came up with a handful of business cards, which she handed to Amelia. Then she turned to Elaine. "What's the tune you're humming? It's beautiful."

"Just something we're singing for the Christmas Eve service at St. Barnabas. You should come."

"I will," said Jacki. "I certainly will."

Jacki, having checked on her cakes and satisfying herself as to their viability, was standing outside chattering with Elaine as Billy hooked the Bobcat to the rear axle, then pulled the car up and out of the ditch.

I paid for my donuts and walked by Roger's cubicle on my way out. He was peering over the top of his half-wall and had viewed the entire episode.

"What just happened?" he said.

I smiled and shrugged and went out the front door to my truck.

And that's how it started.

Chapter 9

"What am I doing here?" I asked, looking around the lobby. "I don't even like this woman."

"Just go in with me," said Pete. "It isn't going to kill you, and besides, I hate going into nursing homes by myself."

The Sunridge Assisted Living facility is located between Blowing Rock and St. Germaine. It's not a top-of-the-line nursing home, but it's okay. The gathering area smelled vaguely of rubbing alcohol, camphor, menthol, and other odors best not ruminated over. There were a number of residents gathered in the room: some around tables, playing cards, dominos, or working puzzles; a few gathered in front of a TV watching CNN; two or three sitting by themselves, either reading, or, in the case of Bessie Baker, scooted up in front of an old spinet piano in her wheelchair.

She was playing slowly and deliberately. A Chopin piece I recognized as *Fantaisie-Impromptu,* easily identifiable by its memorable melody purloined for a popular tune, *I'm Always Chasing Rainbows*. Pauli Girl McCollough was standing behind the piano, listening, her elbows resting on the lid. She waved to us as we came in.

Pete and I walked to the piano and stood politely while she finished the piece. Pete applauded. Bessie glowered at him from beneath unplucked, heavy white eyebrows.

"What do you two want?" she said.

Bessie Baker was small, smaller than I remembered, but then again, I hadn't seen her for fifteen years or so. Her hair was snow white and still thick, although now cut very short. The last time I'd seen her, her hair had been in a bun at the nape of her neck. Her bright blue eyes were clear, but her color wasn't good. Her mouth was nothing more than a slit, turned down at both ends.

"Hi, Miss Baker," said Pete. "I just came over to visit for a bit. You might not remember me ..."

"I remember you perfectly well, Mr. Moss," she said in a dry voice. "I assumed you'd be in prison by this time."

"Nah," said Pete. "They couldn't prove anything."

If Miss Baker got the joke, she didn't let on.

I stuck out my hand. "You remember me as well?" I said. "I wasn't one of your students ..."

"I know you, Hayden Konig." She ignored my outstretched hand. "What are you two doing here?"

"Pete came to visit, Miss Bessie," said Pauli Girl. "He was telling us down at the café about what a great English teacher you were. I invited him up to say hello."

"And I brought Hayden," Pete said.

"Well, hello and goodbye," said Bessie. She turned back to the piano and began playing another piece. Beethoven I thought, but it was difficult to tell.

Pauli Girl gave us the stink-eye and motioned for us to continue the conversation, such as it was.

"You know, Miss Baker," said Pete, fishing for words, "you were probably the best teacher I ever had."

Bessie stopped playing and glared at him. "How the devil would you know? You were asleep in the back row for the entire year. What are you doing here? Really?"

"It was my idea," I fibbed. "I just wanted to ask you a couple of questions."

Bessie's eyes narrowed.

"I wonder if you were in St. Germaine in 1942? Christmas Eve to be exact?"

Her expression turned to a glare.

"I know that you're a long-time member of St. Barnabas, but, as you know, the church burned a few years ago, and all the records were lost. I don't exactly know when you joined the church, but Wynette thinks it might have been around that time." Okay, a small white lie, but in my defense, I'm a cop. I'm used to interrogating suspects. I paused for a moment, hoping Bessie would offer some information, but she didn't. "Did you happen to sing with the choir?" I ventured.

Bessie backed her wheelchair away from the piano.

"I wasn't in the choir."

"Can you tell me what happened on that Christmas Eve? There was a cantata that was scheduled to be sung, but as far as we can tell, it was never performed."

"I don't remember," she said. She spun her chair in a tight circle and rolled it toward a pair of double doors at the end of the room. Pete, Pauli Girl, and I watched in silence as the automatic doors swung open and Bessie Baker wheeled herself down the corridor.

"That went well," said Pete.

"She knows what happened," I said. "And she may be the only one."

"Merry Christmas, Hayden," chirped Helen Pigeon. She was walking across the frozen tundra of Sterling Park, loaded down with packages. "Done your shopping yet?"

"Not yet," I answered. "How are you this afternoon, Helen?" I was a little surprised by Helen's festive disposition. It was just yesterday that I saw

Helen grab the clerk in Schrecker's Jewelry Store by the lapels and shake her like a terrier with a dead squirrel. Brittney Jo had gift-wrapped a package using *regular* cellophane tape instead of *magic transparent* cellophane tape. "*What were you thinking?!*" screamed Helen as the woman's head rattled back and forth. It took both Mr. Schrecker and myself to pull her off the poor woman, who then tried to retaliate by reaching under the counter for her canister of pepper spray. Luckily, it was empty since Brittney Jo had already used it on several customers in the past few days, and what might have been another shopping-related tragedy was averted.

"I'm great," said Helen. "No, better than that. Wonderful! I've just been over to Schrecker's."

I froze. "Are there some bodies I should know about?"

Helen laughed. "No, silly! It's the oddest thing. I was over at the Ginger Cat for lunch and just in the worst mood. You know ... the holiday grumps. I was talking to Annie about something or other, and then Georgia came in from Eden Books next door. The next thing you know, we're laughing and chatting about our kids, and singing funny Christmas carols." A look of confusion crossed Helen's face. "It was weird."

"Yeah," I agreed. "Weird."

"Annie and Georgia told me about your special music on Christmas Eve. It sounds wonderful! I can't wait to hear it."

"I think it's going to be good," I said.

"Anyway, I felt sort of guilty about yesterday, so I decided to go over to Schrecker's and apologize, and take Brittney Jo a jar of cherry preserves that I picked up at the Ginger Cat while I was there. She couldn't have been nicer. She and Luke are coming to our Christmas open-house on Saturday."

"Wow," I said.

"You and Meg are coming, aren't you? I found a fabulous new caterer this morning. She's all the rage."

"Umm ... I can't say for sure. Meg is in charge of our holiday calendar."

"Well, of course she is! I'll give her a call, just in case she forgot. Bye now! Merry Christmas!"

Helen almost skipped across the park.

Something was happening.

Our rehearsal on Thursday night went well. We knocked out the second movement of the cantata and reworked the first.

"This is just wonderful," Rebecca said. "I know the poem, but I've not ever sung anything using a text by Sara Teasdale. Do you think that the composer might have known her?"

The second movement was on a poem entitled *Stars*. It began with a marvelously haunting duet between the two bassoons. They were soon joined by the oboe carrying the melody, and by the time the choir came in two pages later, the mood was magical. And *this* was just with organ accompaniment. With the instruments added, I knew the effect would be spine-tingling.

Alone in the night
On a dark hill
With pines around me
Spicy and still,

And a heaven full of stars
Over my head,

White and topaz
And misty red;

Myriads with beating
Hearts of fire
That aeons
Cannot vex or tire;

Up the dome of heaven
Like a great hill,
I watch them marching
Stately and still,
And I know that I
Am honored to be
Witness
Of so much majesty.

"I've no idea if the composer knew her," I said, "but I think she certainly was a fan. Elle de Fournier not only set this poem, but another one in the last movement as well."

"I've never heard of her," said Phil Camp.

"Sara Teasdale lived in St. Louis, but moved to New York in the 1930s," Rebecca said. Rebecca was the town librarian and well versed in poetry. "She committed suicide, I think, but she was very influential and celebrated in the twenties and thirties."

"Popular with the girls," said Pete. "At least when I was in high school. They were always memorizing Sara Teasdale poems for English class. I was more an Edgar Allan Poe type of guy. You know, 'Quoth the raven, nevermore.'"

"I can just picture the shepherds looking up into the heavens on that night," Elaine said.

"Can we sing it again?" asked Marjorie. "Just one more time? I tell you, I can't get enough of this stuff."

Chapter 10

She delivered her cantata to Mr. Dearman, the choirmaster, at the beginning of November. He had specified the date, and even though she hadn't worked out the final movement, what she'd finished was enough for the choirmaster to get started on. Besides, she told herself, the alternate suggestion she'd provided for the ending would be fine for the premiere. She'd work out the final version later and have the whole thing completed by Christmas at the latest. It would be a present. Accompanying the score she gave to Mr. Dearman was a letter from Nadia Boulanger expressing her delight that one of her favorite pupils was composing again and that she was sure the premiere of La Chanson d'Adoration would be a wonderful success. The choirmaster was thrilled. The singers were thrilled. Everyone was thrilled. Rehearsals started almost immediately, although not really in earnest until after Thanksgiving.

The choir sounded good, she thought, and Stan Dearman had arranged for musicians to drive up from Asheville for the performance. The Christmas Eve service was scheduled for 10:30 in the evening and would last well past midnight, but the cantata would begin at ten o'clock. A pre-service concert.

It was a Thursday, she'd remember in years to come. Christmas Eve. The dress rehearsal had gone splendidly the previous evening, and the weather forecast (always a concern in late December) was for a clear, although cold, night. Perfect, she thought.

At three o'clock in the afternoon, she was fixing herself a cup of tea when there was a knock at her front door.

Meg and I decided to drop by her mother's house after choir rehearsal. In truth, we'd been invited for fruitcake and coffee. Many sons-in-law would view an invitation such as this as cruel and unusual punishment, but not me. Not only did I greatly enjoy Ruby's company, I really liked fruitcake, especially the homemade kind that had been soaked in rum for six months.

"Oh, I almost forgot," said Ruby, once we were seated at the kitchen table, our whipped cream topped fruitcake placed delectably in front of us. "I have a present for you, Hayden. Let me get it."

She disappeared into the living room and came back a moment later with a wrapped box the size of a large book. I'd known Ruby longer than I'd known Meg. They were two peas in a pod—same beautiful smiles, same gray-blue eyes that conveyed a wicked sense of humor—and although Ruby's hair was now silver, one trip to Noylene's Beautifery and they might be taken for sisters. She handed me the wrapped box.

"What's this?" I said. "It's not Christmas yet."

"I thought you could make use of this present ahead of time."

"So I should open it?"

"Absolutely!" said Ruby.

I removed the wrapping paper and looked down at a box of hand-rolled, authentic, one hundred percent Cuban cigars. Fifty *Romeo y Julieta*s. Illegal in every state.

"*Mother!*" said Meg. "You know how I feel about cigars!"

"Wow!" I said. "This is incredible!"

"I got them from a gentleman friend that I met in Miami last summer," said Ruby. "He's Cuban."

"Mother!" said Meg again. "Why didn't you tell me?"

Ruby put on her most innocent expression. "I don't tell you everything, dear. Now eat your fruitcake."

"Don't worry," I said to Meg, conscious of the smile plastered across my face. "I won't smoke them all the first day."

"Humph," said Meg.

We ate our fruitcake and I filled Ruby in on the mystery of the Christmas cantata. Ruby always liked a good mystery.

"So you went and visited this English teacher at the nursing home?" Ruby said.

"Pete and I did," I said. "I shot a few questions at her. I think she knows more than she's saying. She just doesn't want to tell me."

"Why not?"

I shrugged. "She's never liked me much, I guess. Maybe that's it. When she was active at the church, she complained about the music all the time. But that was fifteen years ago."

"She had a lot of musical opinions, did she?"

"I guess."

Ruby laughed. "And you call yourself a detective."

"What?" I said.

"Elle de Fournier?" Ruby said. "How's your French, anyway?"

"Not as good as my German," I admitted.

"Fournier is French ... for 'baker.'"

It took me a second or two to make the connection. "You think?"

It was Meg's turn. "What?" she said, looking first at me, then at her mother.

"Elle ... Elisabeth ... Bessie," said Ruby.

"Elle de Fournier," I said. "Bessie Baker. Baker the Grade Shaker."

86

Chapter 11

"Mozart, isn't it?" I asked, when the music stopped.

Bessie Baker didn't look up from the spinet, but instead started the next movement of the sonata. The slow movement. "It is," she said.

"You play it very well."

We were alone in the gathering area of the nursing home. I supposed that the rest of the residents were in the cafeteria at breakfast. I'd come into the lobby and signed in as a visitor. Hearing the piano, I walked into the main room and stood several paces behind.

"Nonsense," she said, concentrating on the dingy ivory keys. "The first movement was about half speed and you know it. My fingers are almost a century old. What do you want, Hayden?"

She still had a good ear. I was pretty sure she never saw me come in and she'd only heard me speak once in the past fifteen years.

"I came over to tell you that the church choir is singing your cantata on Christmas Eve."

She stopped playing, removed her fingers from the keys, and slowly shut the keyboard lid.

"My cantata?"

"I believe so." I moved to a nearby chair and sat down. "I may be wrong. The style is distinctly American modernist. Written in the '30s or '40s, I'd say, even though the name of the composer is French. Elle de Fournier."

"You think this 'Elle de Fournier' is me?" She rolled her wheelchair backward away from the piano and spun it to face my chair.

"I do."

"And how, pray tell, did you come to this absurd conclusion?"

"Elementary," I said.

"Oh, puhlease! Spare me your juvenile literary allusions."

Pauli Girl came into the room, spotted us right away and came over.

"You obviously have musical training. A lot. People don't play the Mozart sonatas, especially No. 18, from memory, no matter how slowly, unless they have some chops. Added to that, I looked back over some of the letters you wrote to Father Tony complaining about the music at the church after I was hired." I pulled out my small, black notebook and opened it. "And I quote," I said, reading. "Totally ignores dynamic traditions ... ill equipped to deal with the nuances of the French literature ..." I turned a page. "The musical aestheticism of a Philistine ... heavy-handed, ham-fisted, hymn playing suitable only for tent revivals and Methodist services." I closed the notebook and slipped it back into my pocket. "Those are pretty specific criticisms."

Bessie folded her hands and placed them in her lap. "Well ... I do have a way with words."

"Second," I said, "two of the movements are composed on texts of Sara Teasdale. Pete Moss mentioned that the girls in his, or rather *your*, English class always memorized poems by Sara Teasdale. Now, granted, she's an important poet of the early 20th century, but in my experience, the teacher tends to steer the impressionable student towards what they themselves enjoy."

Pauli Girl was paying rapt attention.

Bessie thought for a moment. "Yes," she granted. "Your pedagogical assumption may have validity. Sara Teasdale is a particular favorite of mine."

"Third, Elle de Fournier equals Bessie Baker. Not that much of a stretch, although I'll admit that it was Ruby Farthing who pointed me in the right direction. I should have gotten it earlier, but my French is poor, and it never occurred to me that the composer might still be alive, not to mention that I might be able to talk to her."

Bessie sighed heavily. "So what do you want from me?"

"It *is* you?" asked Pauli Girl.

"Of course it is!" Bessie snapped. "Try to keep up, child."

"I have some questions," I said. "About the score, but also about the premiere performance."

"I don't want to talk about either one," said Bessie.

"But, Miss Baker," interrupted Pauli Girl, "you *have to*. Here's the thing. That music is changing people. All over town!"

Bessie Baker looked at Pauli Girl as if deciding whether to believe her or not. Her lower lip quivered ever so slightly. Then she put her hands on the wheels of her chair and pushed herself toward the hallway.

"Rubbish!" she said, over her shoulder.

A late breakfast at the Slab was just the thing for a Friday morning in December. I got back into town at about 9:30, parked my truck in front of the police station, and walked the half block to the restaurant on the corner. The breakfast crowd was all but gone. Nancy was there, though, and Dave, holding down our table in the back. Cynthia was leaning against the counter wiping her brow with a napkin. Pete had collapsed at another table and was sprawled in a chair, a coffee cup balanced in his hand. Noylene, behind the counter, was running a cleaning rag over everything, a model of efficiency. I expected Meg to join us. I'd called her from my cell on my way back to town and left her a message.

"I done sold all my wreaths," said Noylene, gesturing to the empty wall that, as recently as yesterday afternoon, had been laden with her holiday wreaths, festooned with an infinite variety of trinkets, pine cones, ribbons and spray-on snow. A particular favorite seems to have been her signature "Santa at the Manger" wreath that featured a bright plastic rendering of the two main subjects (Santa on his knees, praying, and the infant Jesus looking up from his manger with a startled expression on his face), encircled by toy animals that Noylene had bought at the Atlanta Zoo when she'd been there on vacation last summer. Noylene didn't hold with using only barnyard animals, and although the cows, sheep, and donkeys were there as a nod toward tradition, Noylene's Christmas menagerie included warthogs, penguins, polar bears, meerkats, hedgehogs, and emus. "If Santa could show up at the manger," she said to any detractors, "so could the emus."

"Shoot, Noylene," said Cynthia. "I didn't even get one. I waited too long, I guess."

"You snooze, you lose," said Noylene. "There's still a week and a half till Christmas. I could prob'ly sell another dozen if I could get any more of them praying Santas, but I can't. I order them from Japan. That's why that baby Jesus is wearing a kimono."

The cowbell tied to the front door of the Slab banged against the glass a moment later, announcing Meg's arrival.

"Is there any food left?" she asked as she took off her coat and hung it on one of the wall hooks. I'd dropped mine over the back of an empty chair.

"Not much," admitted Pete. "I can rustle you up an omelet or something."

"We're out of eggs," said Cynthia. "Chicken eggs, anyway. I think there're some duck eggs left."

"What?" said Meg. "No, thank you. I do not care for duck eggs."

Manuel came out of the kitchen, wiping his hands on his apron. "Miss Meg! How nice to see you!"

"Have we got anything left in the kitchen?" asked Pete.

"Hmm," said Manuel. He smiled at Meg, dropped his apron, and rubbed his hands together. "For you, a breakfast couscous with a fresh fruit compote."

"Really?" asked Meg. "Hayden, too?"

"*Sí*. You will love it," said Manuel with a big grin. "Couscous cooked with butter and cinnamon; topped with a compote of peaches, cherries, cranberries; and apples simmered in brown sugar, lemon juice. Oh, yes. The secret ingredient—a tea bag of orange pekoe. I do take the tea bag out."

"Hey! Can I have that, too?" called Dave from the back table.

"Eat your goose eggs, Dave," said Nancy.

"Duck eggs," said Dave miserably. "They sort of taste like dirt."

"Well, come on, sit down," Pete said, motioning to Meg and me. "Give us the scoop."

Meg and I took two of the empty seats at the table with Dave and Nancy. Pete dragged his chair across the floor and joined us. Cynthia came over with the coffee pot, sat down and made herself comfortable. She filled her own cup, then passed the pot around to everyone.

"So I went to see Bessie Baker," I said. "This morning, first thing. She was playing the piano when I walked in." I took a sip of coffee.

"And then?" said Meg.

I put my cup down. "And then I mentioned to her that I thought she might be the composer of the Christmas cantata."

"What did she say?" asked Meg.

"In the face of all the evidence, she admitted it."

"Well, if that don't wash the hog's back legs!" said Pete. "Did you ask her about the 1942 performance?"

"Sure I did," I said. "She said she wouldn't talk about it, then she rolled away."

"Rolled away?" asked Cynthia.

"Wheelchair," said Pete.

"Oh."

"Why don't you use your so-called charms on her?" asked Nancy. "Maybe you could draw her out. She's been there for so long ..."

"Alone," added Meg. "I checked. She hasn't had any visitors for years."

"Well, it's no wonder, as crabby as she is," said Pete. "Who'd bother?"

"We should bother," said Meg. "*We* should bother."

Chapter 12

The third Sunday of Advent marked the advance of the Christmas woodpeckers. Two woodpeckers had gotten into the sanctuary of St. Barnabas sometime between Friday evening and Sunday morning. The sexton had cleaned the church on Friday afternoon and all was fine. The altar guild didn't notice anything out of the ordinary when they were decorating on Saturday, but then again, Joyce Cooper pointed out that they didn't bother to check the Chrismon tree.

The tree, being made primarily of green pipe-cleaners, contained no actual wood, but must have looked real enough to attract the two birds. Once ensconced in the plastic branches, they were delighted to discover that there were beetles living in the Styrofoam Chrismon decorations.

One day last summer, just after Wendy had taken care of her possum infestation, she went down into her basement and discovered wood beetles scrabbling across the floor joists of her house. She called the exterminator to have him take care of the problem. Unfortunately, when she was cleaning out the basement so the exterminator could do his job, she moved the box of Chrismons to the new storage room at St. Barnabas. The possums had gaily chomped through the top layer of Chrismons, devouring beetles as they went, but the remainder of the pests had been inadvertently transported to the church.

The good news was that the woodpeckers had finally taken care of the beetle problem.

The bad news was that the Chrismon tree looked as though it had been hit by a small meteor.

Once the Chrismons had been pulverized to powder, the woodpeckers turned their attention to the plastic foliage. What was left were streams of sad gold ribbon, a large pile of Styro-rubble, scattered plastic pearls, pipe-cleaners strewn hither and yon, and a tree that was leaning crazily on what was left of its trunk. The two woodpeckers were sitting politely above the mess on one of the huge cross beams that spanned the roof of the nave.

Once the disaster had been discovered, a group of us gathered to survey the damage and contemplate the problem.

"How are we going to get them down?" asked Father Ward Shavers, pointing at the birds. "We can't let them tear up all the wood in the sanctuary."

"Agreed," said Bev. "Hayden?"

"Well, I guess we could call Billy and have him take care of them."

"I don't want them killed," said Gina Shavers.

"Right," agreed Kimberly Walnut. "They're Christmas wood-peckers."

A little girl and her mother wandered up. They were too early for church, but too late for Sunday School. "What happened to the church's Christmas tree?" asked the girl.

"Chrismon tree," Kimberly Walnut corrected.

The girl looked at her, confusion on her face. Kimberly Walnut, sensing a "teaching moment," was gearing up to explain to the three year old why we couldn't have a Christmas tree in church during Advent, but it was okay to have one covered in beetle-infested Styrofoam. Mercifully, Mark Wells jumped in.

"Woodpeckers got it," he said, shaking his head in mock-dismay. "Terrible, terrible woodpeckers."

The little girl turned to her mother. "Are they going to get ours, too?" she asked, worry evident in her tiny voice.

"Probably," said Mark. "Once they get a taste ..."

"Don't listen to him," said Gina. "Of course they won't. They're right up there, see?" She pointed to the rafters and the little girl's gaze followed her finger. "We'll get them outside and let them go."

"Why don't we worry about the woodpeckers *after* the service?" I suggested. "Maybe clean up this mess. We only have a few minutes." I looked around at the destruction. "That's it for the Chrismon tree faction, I suppose."

"Another doctrinal schism prevented by woodpeckers," said Mark. "I believe it also happened in 1378 when a woodpecker killed the anti-pope and saved the church. That's why Pope Clementine the sixteenth has a woodpecker on his coat-of-arms."

"Really?" asked Gina.

"Oh, absolutely," said Mark. "I can pretty much guarantee that's what happened."

The service began and there were a lot of folks in attendance. This was typical of St. Barnabas, as it was in most churches. The closer we got to Christmas, the more people showed up. So with just one more Sunday to go until the big day, I'd gone with Meg's suggestion (and the priest's blessing) and slipped a couple of innocuous Christmas hymns into the mix. *Love Came Down at Christmas* and *Of the Father's Love Begotten* might be gotten away with when coupled with *On Jordan's Bank, the Baptist's Cry* and *Lo, He Comes With Clouds Descending*. Next Sunday was Christmas Eve as well as the fourth

Sunday of Advent, and we'd be singing full-blown carols both in the morning and in the evening services.

Our anthem at the offering, the first movement of the cantata, went splendidly. There was the absence of the accompanying instruments to deal with, but I covered most of the parts from the organ. The congregation sat in rapt silence as the final chord echoed through the space.

"Beautiful!" whispered Meg. I looked across the choir. Every member was grinning ear to ear.

The only disruption in the service happened during communion when one of the woodpeckers (obviously no fan of Brahms) took offense at the choir singing *The White Dove* and began to tap a tarantella on the beam on which it was resting.

"Use your gun," suggested Marjorie, as soon as the motet was over.

"No, don't!" said Rebecca. "You'll scare the clergy."

"I wasn't going to," I said. "Anyway, Billy's coming by later to take care of the problem."

We sang the last hymn, *Lo, He Comes,* with full organ, descant, and *en chamade* trumpets.

"Go in peace, to love and serve the Lord," announced the priest.

And we did.

Chapter 13

Meg started the ball rolling by telling Georgia. Georgia was in the Bear and Brew having lunch and she told Gwen Jackson, the vet, who was standing behind her at the check-out register. Gwen was going to the Piggly Wiggly for cat food, and while she was there, told Hannah and Grace, the two checkout girls. Meanwhile, Noylene had overheard the entire conversation at the Slab and conveyed it to all concerned at the Beautifery. That was all it took. Before three o'clock on Monday, everyone in town knew that Old Miss Baker was a composer and that the St. Barnabas choir would be premiering her cantata on Christmas Eve. Not only that, but she was single-handedly responsible for a woodpecker infestation, and rumored to have millions of dollars in a secret bank account in the Cayman Islands. Such was the power of the grapevine in St. Germaine.

The *St. Germaine Tattler,* never a newspaper to print an untruth if they could get to the bottom of something, called Meg to get the whole scoop. She was glad to fill them in, and on Tuesday morning, everyone knew the rumor about the bank account was unfounded, that Bessie Baker had been a world-class composer, and that the long-delayed world premiere of her Christmas work *La Chanson d'Adoration* would happen this Sunday, December 24th. No mention was made of the woodpeckers.

The paper found a picture of Bessie Baker in their files, an old one from the 1970s, taken at her retirement dinner, and they ran it with the story. Meg had added the "hook" that the paper was always after, mentioning that Bessie Baker, beloved teacher, had been sitting by herself in the nursing home for five long years. No friends, no visitors ... nothing. For a

97

town that was now hooked on Christmas, the story was all it took.

Suddenly, Miss Baker's former students were dropping by Sunridge Assisted Living bringing cookies, introducing their children to the old lady, and then bestowing small gifts on whomever they might see shuffling down the hall, since Bessie Baker refused each and every one of them. Bevies of Christmas carolers made the trip over from town and serenaded all the residents. Miss Baker made a point of ignoring them. The Kiwanis Club brought a pickup-truck-load of decorations and decked the halls from the carpet to the ceiling tiles. The high school band director decided that a reprise of their Christmas concert was in order. The place was a beehive of activity, and the staff, as well as most of the residents, loved it.

Bessie Baker hated it.

At least that's what she told me when I stopped by in the middle of the week.

"I hope you're happy," she snarled. "I hate this."

"What?" I asked her.

"People are bothering me all day long. I just want a little peace and quiet."

"Well, you can't blame them, really. You've had a profound influence on many of these people, both when you were teaching, and through your composition."

"Bah!"

I shrugged. "I'm telling you, this music changed the whole town. Make of it what you want. You have a gift. That cantata is something special."

"That's ridiculous. I don't care one whit about that thing. I've had nothing to do with music for the past sixty years. "

"You play the piano," I said. "That's not nothing."

"It's something to do while I wait to die," she said. "Someone donated it a few months ago. Didn't even bother to have it tuned."

"I can get that done for you."

"Save your money," she snapped. "I won't be playing anymore."

"That's a shame. Anyway, I came over because I just have a few questions about the music ..."

She didn't answer.

"Fair enough. But since you don't care anything about your cantata, I guess you wouldn't mind if I made a few changes. Just a few. For instance, it's very tough to find *one* bassoon player on Christmas Eve, not to mention *two*. I think a bass clarinet might work just as well. They play in the same range, after all, and I'd keep the overall woodwind timbre intact."

She didn't answer.

I walked over to the piano, sat down, and raised the key cover. Then I put the score I'd brought onto the music stand and opened it.

"Did you mean to keep this G-natural all the way from measure 23 to measure 39? I know that's what it says, but there's a G# in the pedal of the organ part. Maybe it's a copyist error. Listen."

I played a few measures with the G-natural, then played them again substituting a G#.

"See what I mean?"

She didn't answer.

"Also," I said, turning a few pages, "the choir's having some difficulty with this canonic section in the third movement." I played through the choral parts.

Rise up, my love, my fair one, and come away.
For, lo, the winter is past, the rain is over and gone;
The flowers appear on the earth;
the time of the singing of birds is come,
and the voice of the turtle is heard in our land.

"See?" I said. "A four part canon at the seventh? That's too hard for us to sing unaccompanied. I'm just going to use the instruments to double the vocal parts. Now here on page 56 ..."

"*Don't you dare!*" she hissed, showing me her yellowed teeth. "Don't you *dare,* Hayden Konig! And don't think I'm fooled for one instant. I know *exactly* what you're doing!"

I looked at her from the piano, a small smile playing on my lips.

"Very well," she said. "You obviously won't leave. Ask your questions."

Chapter 14

Two men stood at her front door, both in uniform, their hats tucked under their arms. One of them had a letter in his other hand. She knew why they were there just as she knew what the letter said. They declined her wooden invitation to come in, handed her the envelope, but broke the news to her in person. Henry had been killed on the 22nd of December—two days earlier in Tunisia at the battle of Longstop Hill. He was a hero, the lieutenant said. A credit to his unit, the 18th division, and his country. She barely heard him. There would be some life insurance, the other one said. She nodded in mute despair.

They asked if she had someone she could call. No, she answered. She had no phone, but if they would give the message to his parents, she would count it as a great kindness. They agreed, and she gave them the address. The two soldiers conveyed their sorrow at her loss once more, left her front porch, got into their car, and drove away down the dusty dirt road.

She closed the front door, walked into her living room, and collapsed.

Her friend Mary Alice was the one who found her. Mary Alice had gotten the news from her mother, who happened to be at the Greenaways' house when the two soldiers arrived. When she heard the terrible account, Mary Alice picked up her skirts and raced to Bessie's house as fast as her sturdy legs would carry her. A glass of water and some smelling salts brought Bessie around, but did nothing to stem her grief. Her sobs echoed through the house.

The cantata was cancelled. Henry Greenaway and his family had been members of the church for years and he was the first of her sons to perish in the Great War. It was a devastating blow. The midnight service that Christmas Eve was conducted as usual, but most of the choir was absent and it was a "said" service. No hymns or carols echoed through that cold, still night. Many of the parishioners, those who had heard the tragic news, chose to stay home, even though they might have found comfort in the priest's message that evening. Mary Alice stayed with Bessie and heard the account of the service from her mother the next day.

"So there was no performance?" I asked.

"Not then, not ever," answered Bessie Baker, in a clipped, matter-of-fact voice. "The choirmaster and I talked about doing it the following year, but then, in the course of our conversations, he decided that I might be a grieving widow in need of some comfort. He didn't care for my rebuff and that was the end of that. He was called up for service a few months later, and shipped out before Easter. I later heard that he was killed in Germany."

She paused for a long moment. "I have no use for this composing foolishness and I do not appreciate you dragging this thing back out."

"I'm sorry," I said. "Sorry about your husband, but also sorry there was no performance. It's an extraordinary work. If someone had heard it perhaps ..."

Henry's family was supportive, as far as they could be to an unknown daughter-in-law of eight months, but they withdrew into their own grief and gradually pulled away from her. She had Henry's house and the life insurance, but his parents were less generous when it came to their business holdings. She was not considered part of the family. If there had been a child, perhaps, but that hadn't happened. Estranged from the Greenaways, within a year she'd sold the house and moved back to Asheville. She wouldn't touch a piano again for over sixty years.

Bessie took back her maiden name and began teaching English. Twelve years later, her parents were killed in an automobile accident, and when a position opened at St. Germaine High School, she took it. Her friend Mary Alice had left the town years before. The Greenaways were gone as well. No one in town recognized her and she didn't remind them, discouraging friendships, keeping acquaintances at arm's length, choosing instead to keep to herself. She cultivated a caustic wit and used it mercilessly on unprepared students, ill-equipped teachers, and ineffectual administrators. She was feared. Her mouth set itself in a permanent scowl and the lines in her face deepened as she became the crone of the village. The days turned to months, and then to years, and then to scores of years. Now she could see the end.

"I'm not sorry about dragging your cantata back out, though," I said. "It's changed everyone who's sung it."

Bessie Baker put her ancient hands on the wheels of her chair and rolled it toward the exit.

"What about that G-natural?" I called after her. "Measures 23 to 39?"

"You know perfectly well it's a G-natural," she said, without looking back. "But do what you want. I couldn't care less."

Chapter 15

The Jessetonians had their tree up and decorated by the time the woodpeckers had been captured. As an *homage*, they placed two life-sized papier-mâché woodpeckers at the top of the tree in place of the usual turtledoves and vowed they'd be adorning the tree from henceforth.

Billy Hixon, dressed as Santa and holding the large birdcage aloft to display his two prizes, explained to the children in Sterling Park that the only way to catch woodpeckers was to put a little salt on their tails. He was going to take them back to the North Pole where they'd help in the workshop, drilling holes for wooden puppets' noses. Moosey and his friend Bernadette, finally released from the prison of elementary school, spent the rest of the day chasing birds with a couple of salt shakers they'd purloined from the Slab. Unfortunately, they'd caught one fairly early in the exercise, a robin with a bad wing, and then there was no stopping them.

I was practicing my prelude for Sunday morning when Pauli Girl came up the steps, into the loft and down to the organ console. I saw her and stopped playing.

"I had an idea," she said.

"What?"

"Maybe you could have Miss Baker come and hear the cantata."

"I already thought of that," I said. "I asked her to come to the performance, or even a rehearsal, but she said absolutely not. She's not interested."

"She doesn't like to go out at night," said Pauli Girl. "None of the residents do."

"Makes sense," I said.

"But what about something during the day? I think I could take her out if she thought she were going somewhere else. Maybe to the library. Then I'd wheel her into the church, and there you'd be."

"You might just make her mad," I said. "And Bessie Baker's mad is more mad than I want to see."

"Maybe," said Pauli Girl, "but maybe not. She started playing the piano again after you left. I think there's something there."

The fourth movement was easier, and was a setting of another poem by Sara Teasdale. The choir, now familiar with the style and the harmonic language, caught on quickly.

Life has loveliness to sell,
All beautiful and splendid things,
Blue waves whitened on a cliff,
Soaring fire that sways and sings,
And children's faces looking up
Holding wonder like a cup.

Life has loveliness to sell,
Music like a curve of gold,
Scent of pine trees in the rain,
Eyes that love you, arms that hold,
And for your spirit's still delight,
Holy thoughts that star the night.

"Wow!" said Marjorie. "I can't wait until Sunday night! This is going to be great."

"It's going to be sad when it all ends," said Rebecca. "I've been singing this in my head for two weeks straight."

"Is Miss Baker coming to the performance?" asked Martha.

I shook my head. "She doesn't care to attend. She's not exactly thrilled that we're doing it."

"Why not?" asked Muffy. "If someone sang a song I wrote, boy, I'd be happy!"

"Me, too," agreed Goldi Fawn. "I remember when I wrote *Suckin' Christmas Dinner Through a Straw* and Louise Mandrell was gonna sing it. I was all set to go to Dollywood and hear her, but she had to cancel when her pet pig got hit by a car."

"Miss Baker has her reasons," I said. "She's been through a lot."

"Is that the end of the piece?" asked Rhiza Walker, flipping through a couple more blank pages at the end of her score. "It doesn't seem like the end."

"It's not," I said. "The composer gives instructions for the singing of a carol after the last movement. *I Wonder as I Wander*. You'll find the music in the back of your folder."

"Is that a solo?" asked Muffy hopefully.

"No," I said. "Sorry. There *are* a couple of solo parts. I thought that they probably used the choral version that John Jacob Niles wrote. It would have been the right time period."

"Did Niles write it?" asked Sheila. "I thought I remembered that it was an Appalachian folk song."

"He 'collected' it," I said. "He heard a fragment and made a carol out of it. That was his story, anyway."

"Can we audition?" asked Muffy.

"Nope," I said. "Tiff's singing the alto solo and Bert's singing the tenor."

"Oh," said Muffy, "that's okay, then. I don't sing alto."

We sang through the anthem, worked on it for twenty minutes or so, and I proclaimed it ready for prime time.

"We'll sing this as the anthem in the morning service on Sunday," I said. "It's not often that Christmas Eve falls on a Sunday. We're also doing the *St. James Christmas Service* music for both the morning service and the midnight mass. The cantata will be before the service. We'll begin at 10:30."

"Everyone's coming," said Cynthia. "The whole town, I think."

"Probably not the whole town," corrected Pete. "But a mess of people."

"I'll let Billy know," said Elaine. "They're going to have to put up a lot of chairs."

"I've been telling everyone at the Beautifery," said Goldi Fawn Birtwhistle. "As soon as I read their stars, I tell them they should be here on Christmas Eve. It's just good karma."

"What time do we need to be here?" asked Codfish.

"Ten o'clock would be good," I answered. "We can warm up and go over the service. Now about dress rehearsal. I'd like to change it from Saturday afternoon at three to Saturday afternoon at two. All the instrumentalists can be here. Is that okay with everyone?"

"I think most of us were going to be here anyway. We're decorating," said Georgia. "Starting at noon."

"We'll plan on it," I said. "Now let's sing the entire cantata one time through, start to finish, no stopping."

"Including *I Wonder as I Wander*?" asked Phil.

"Sure," I said.

I began the prelude, covering the instrumental parts as best I could, giving the choir an idea of what would be in store for them when the players arrived.

We pushed ahead and sang through the movements, ending with the carol.

When we finished, a hush fell over the church. No choir member said anything and I could see more than a few glistening eyes. They got up, one by one, and in silence, made their way down the stairs and out of the front doors into the cold, cold, starry night.

Chapter 16

On the Saturday before Christmas, St. Germaine was always packed, and this day was no exception. The hustle and bustle downtown was worthy of any Christmas movie ever staged. The decorations had come out in full force as soon as the Christmas crabbiness had stopped. We'd had some decorating going on previously—decorating the shops on the square was, after all, a town ordinance—but folks had been chintzy. A wreath here, a sad strand of cheap blinking lights there. Now the square was in full Christmas bloom. Lights abounded. Garlands, bows, ribbons, and ornaments were the order of the day. Even Noylene's wreaths made appearances here and there to great acclaim. The Rotary Club's Christmas Crèche was up in the park, the last performance scheduled for this evening. It was a beauty. A stable that would be the envy of any miniature chalet in Switzerland. If Joseph and Mary could have stayed in a stable like this, they wouldn't have been so quick to head to Egypt. Kids were gathered around the stalls, enjoying the farm animals that Seymour Krebbs was always happy to provide and supervise on the last Saturday: a Christmas petting zoo, and it was full, of animals and children.

We spent the morning in the town, Nancy, Dave, and I, making our police presence known, although it was hardly necessary. Nancy had to have stern words with a woman who wanted to take a picture of her son sitting on Jeremiah the donkey. When Dave caught a boy eating a candy cane he hadn't paid for, Dave shook his finger sternly at the lad, tousled his hair, and gave the shopkeeper a quarter.

"Dave," said Nancy, "did you just tousle that lad's hair? *Tousle*?"

"Why, yes," said Dave proudly. "I believe I did."

"Holy smokes," said Nancy. "I think I'm in Bedford Falls."

Meg joined me for lunch in the park, even though it was cold. We enjoyed a thermos of homemade chicken soup and watched the festivities. There was a caroling group, dressed as Dickens characters, making their way around the square, stopping to sing at different shops. A group of teenagers in marching band uniforms were successfully hawking fund-raising candy bars. There was even a Santa Claus making his rounds. The scene was altogether charming.

At one o'clock, I headed to the church, as I felt I should probably make some attempt at preparation. The church was abuzz with people, decorating and preparing the sanctuary for Christmas. At 1:30 the choir began to arrive. At two o'clock, the choir loft was full, and the decorators began to disappear and leave us to our rehearsal.

I had decided not to play, but rather to conduct the small ensemble and the choir. Since there was an organ part, I'd called my friend from Lenoir to play. Edna Terra-Pocks had a Master's degree in organ from Yale and we'd gone over the piece beforehand. She'd also played at St. Barnabas for a number of months as a substitute and knew the organ well. I wasn't worried about her in the least.

I *was* worried about one of the bassoonists. Henry Iman played very well but had a propensity towards the bottle. If we could get him to the church, it shouldn't be a problem, as he played as well inebriated as the second bassoonist did sober. The trick was making sure he showed up, and showed up with his instrument. I put Marjorie in charge. Not only was she responsible for getting him to the rehearsal, but on Christmas Eve, she was to pick him up at six, take him to her house, and watch him until she brought him to church at 9:45 sharp.

The flute player was a friend of mine from Boone. She'd brought the clarinetist whom I didn't know, but whom she highly recommended. The oboist was Will Purser. Will was the acting teacher at Lees-McRae College in Banner Elk, but was also a fine double-reed player, handling both the oboe and the English horn parts. Five players plus the organ and me as conductor. With chairs, stands, instruments, and our expanded choir, it made for a packed choir loft. Still, after a few minutes of jostling and settling in, we were ready to begin.

In my experience, the first rehearsal with instruments (of any complex piece) is not going to go smoothly. This afternoon was no exception. I had a plan, though, and had met with the players once during the week. They had a good idea of the scope of the piece. The trick was getting the choir to find their entrances and pitches using timbres they weren't accustomed to. It didn't take long, and once the kinks were worked out, everything flowed pretty smoothly. We'd finished the fourth movement, the last that Bessie Baker had written, and I cut the choir off and had them take their seats. Edna, from the organ, looked at me and said, "Who did you say wrote this?"

"Bessie Baker," I said. "She was an English teacher. I'll fill you in later."

"This is ... wow ... beautiful," said Will Purser, the oboist.

"Are we going to sing the carol?" asked Nancy. "*I Wonder as I Wander*?"

"No. We're fine on that," I replied. "We'll concentrate on the movements with instruments."

There was a noise in the narthex, and we heard the double doors at the front of the church open, and then bang closed. A moment later Pauli Girl came down the center aisle pushing a wheelchair in front of her, and in that chair was Miss Bessie Baker. How Pauli Girl had talked her into coming to St. Barnabas, I didn't know.

The choir was silent as Pauli Girl rolled the chair all the way to the front steps of the chancel. Then, slowly, she spun the chair around so Miss Baker could see the choir. The old woman appeared much smaller from the balcony than I remembered her just a few days earlier: a small shriveled form bundled in several blankets.

Pete Moss stood up first and started applauding. Meg joined him immediately. It took a long moment for the rest of the choir to understand what was going on, but when they did, they were on their feet, clapping.

"Who is that?" asked Will.

"That's her," I said. "Bessie Baker."

"Wow," said Will, getting to his feet. "Brava!" he yelled.

"Brava," echoed the choir, as the sound swelled. A full five minutes later, the sound started to abate and the choir looked down at the composer in expectation.

"Let's sing it," I said. "Pick up your music."

It was as good a reading as any dress rehearsal could be. The instrumentalists were wonderfully sensitive. The choir sang as if they were possessed by Lutherans. There were a few bobbles to be sure, but *my*, what a performance. The fourth movement, in my opinion, was the most enchanting of all:

Spend all you have for loveliness,
Buy it and never count the cost;
For one white singing hour of peace
Count many a year of strife well lost,
And for a breath of ecstasy
Give all you have been, or could be.

We sang the last line, heard the instruments finish as the sound of the choir died away, and then stood in silence, looking down at the old woman.

"Well?" she said. She was frail, but her voice still commanded the room.

The choir looked around at each other.

"Well, what?" I called down to her.

"Well, where's the rest?"

"*I Wonder as I Wander*?" I said. "We'd be happy to sing it for you."

"Good Lord, no!" she said loudly. "I hate that carol. Where's the rest of the piece?"

"That's all we have," I said. "That's where it ends. There *is* no more."

"You don't have the last movement?"

"That's all there is," I said.

She turned to Pauli Girl. "Take me home," she said in a hard voice.

"But Miss Baker," said Pauli Girl, "it's not their fault ..."

"And *you*!" Bessie Baker pointed up at me. "I'll expect you at the nursing home in an hour."

I arrived at the Sunridge Assisted Living facility and was met by Pauli Girl when I entered the lobby.

114

"Miss Baker's really anxious," Pauli Girl said after I'd greeted her. "I've never seen her like this."

"Well, let's go and talk to her."

Pauli Girl led the way down the dimly-lit hallway, then stopped and knocked on a nondescript door about halfway down the corridor.

"Come!" barked the voice from the other side.

Pauli Girl opened the door and stood aside as I went into the room ahead of her.

The room had a neatly made bed in one corner covered by a white chenille bedspread. On the opposite wall, there was an antique dresser, and on top of the dresser sat a small TV. Beside the TV, in a silver frame, was a picture of a smiling couple, probably taken sometime in the 1930s or '40s judging by the clothing. The young woman looking back into the room from behind the glass might have been—probably was—Bessie. The man was no one I recognized.

A large hand-made, braided rag rug lay on the floor next to the bed, covering most of the exposed floor area in the room. The parts that weren't covered by the rag rug revealed a worn industrial carpet of no discernible color.

There were two doors and a small window in the room. Pauli Girl was leaning against the door to the hallway where we'd just entered. Hanging on a second door, the door I presumed led to the bathroom, was an old bathrobe.

Bessie Baker was sitting in her wheelchair looking out the window, one hand holding back the tired, blue-checkered curtains. An old, metal Venetian blind had been rattled to the top of the window but was hanging askew. She glanced back at me after a moment and caught me checking out her apartment.

"You're late," she snapped, her disquietude apparent.

"Sorry," I replied. "I had to lock the church up. Put everything away ..."

"Yes, yes. I'm sure you have any number of excuses." She waved a thin arm in my direction as if dismissing the notion that anything not directly related to her wants was of any interest. Then, suddenly, her demeanor changed. She took a deep breath, and visibly relaxed.

"I'm sorry," she said.

I glanced over at Pauli Girl, but there was no change of expression on her face.

"I called you here ..." Bessie said. Then her voice softened. "I *asked* you here ... to give you the last movement of the cantata."

"You have it?" I said.

"Yes, I have it. I finished it in early December of 1942. The choir director didn't want to include it."

"Well," I said, "that was a little close for a premiere."

She nodded. "Possibly. Anyway, I want you to have it. You can use it or not. I know it's late."

Bessie got up out of her chair and walked over to the dresser. She saw my look and said, "Oh, I can walk all right. I do have to use a cane. It's just easier at my age to have someone roll me around."

She opened one of the top drawers, rummaged around for a moment, and came out with a sheaf of pages, handwritten music notation on oversized, cream-colored paper. She walked across the room and handed it to me.

"Here it is."

I looked at the music, then back at Bessie. "Why wasn't it with the rest of the score?"

She pursed her lips, as if trying to find the right words. "I ..." she started. "I didn't want ..." She squared her shoulders and looked me right in the eye. "It was finished too late for the first performance. After Christmas ... Well, I guess it never found its way into the score."

"Would you mind if I included it?" I asked, gently.

"It's up to you," she said.

"Well, I'll certainly see what we can do. I don't know for sure, but we might manage it."

Bessie nodded, but didn't say anything.

"Would you like to play through it for me?" I asked.

If this caught her by surprise, she recovered quickly. "I suppose I could do that. "

Pauli Girl pushed Bessie's wheelchair down to the lobby where the upright piano sat, unused, except for Bessie's occasional forays into her musical past. Pauli Girl pushed her up to the keyboard and I placed the score on the music stand. The old woman's fingers were less nimble than they'd been when she'd first composed it, but she played the piece very well. It was a solo. A solo for mezzo-soprano with English horn and organ: a delicious, sensual melody that, along with its haunting accompaniment, brought the entire cantata to its inevitable finish.

She played the last few measures, then let her fingers rest on the piano keys for a few moments before lifting them off the keyboard, and resting them in her lap.

"Wow!" said Pauli Girl.

"It's quite beautiful," I said. "And I wouldn't say that if it weren't."

"I know you wouldn't," Bessie replied. "That's what I like about you, Hayden Konig."

"That's what you *like*?" I said with a laugh. "I didn't think you liked anything about me."

"You were a pretentious fool when you first came to St. Barnabas. All that Langlais organ music. The Jonathan Harvey *Magnificat*? I mean *really!*"

"Okay, I admit it. But I've gotten better, haven't I?"

"Yes, you have," Bessie said. "You're very good. I should have told you sooner."

"Thank you."

"And I'm deeply grateful that you've revived that old cantata. More than you can appreciate." She smiled. "I've never heard it, you know. Except in my head."

"It's been our pleasure. Do you think you might come to the church to hear the performance?"

"No," she replied. "No, I don't think I'd better. Doctor's orders ..."

"I understand," I said. "I'll make sure we get a recording of the service and I'll bring it by on Monday." I suddenly remembered that Monday was the 25th. "A Christmas present," I said.

"I would like that," she said.

Pauli Girl stayed with Miss Bessie Baker, and I drove back into town, pondering the last movement of her cantata. It was what the work had been missing, and hearing it as she played it, I knew it for what it was. The perfect conclusion to an astonishing composition.

But it was all wrong.

Chapter 17

"I don't get it," I said to Meg. "It's right, but it's all wrong."

Meg and I sat at the Bear and Brew at one of the long tables. The Bear and Brew had an interesting past. It had begun its life as a feed store, been renovated into a great pizza and beer joint, burnt down by the wrath of the Almighty, and now rebuilt to its inglorious splendor using reclaimed, century-old barn wood. It was a concession that the insurance company had made to restore the character of the old place.

Pete and Cynthia sat across from us. Ruby, Meg's mother, joined us as well. Rhiza Walker had the chair at the end. I'd just told them the entire story of Bessie Baker and now I put the manuscript on the table.

"The music is perfect," I said. "But I think she got confused on the text. It's another Sara Teasdale poem, but maybe she's got the wrong one."

"Let me see," said Rhiza, reaching over and picking up the manuscript. She pulled out a pair of zebra-striped reading glasses and put them on the end of her nose.

Pete filled our glasses from the beer pitcher while Rhiza studied the score.

"I think you're right," she said.

"Why don't you read it to us?" suggested Meg.

Rhiza adjusted her reading glasses, and read:

Before you kissed me only winds of heaven
Had kissed me, and the tenderness of rain -
Now you have come, how can I care for kisses
Like theirs again?

I sought the sea, she sent her winds to meet me,
They surged about me singing of the south -
I turned my head away to keep still holy
Your kiss upon my mouth.

I am my love's and he is mine forever,
Sealed with a seal and safe forevermore -
Think you that I could let a beggar enter
Where a king stood before?

Rhiza put down the music and took off her glasses. "I'm not good at sight-reading scores," she admitted. "How does the music sound?"

"It's wonderful," I said. "I'm fairly sure this part was written too late to be included in the original premiere."

"When was it written?" asked Ruby. "Before Christmas?"

I nodded. "Yes. Bessie indicated that she finished it early in December."

"Then it's obvious," said Ruby.

"To you, maybe," said Pete. "Not to me."

"Me, either," said Rhiza.

"Ruby, if you keep solving these mysteries, I'll be putting you on the payroll," I said.

"Well?" said Meg, holding up both hands in a pleading gesture. "*Well?*"

Ruby savored the moment. "This last poem is called *The Kiss*," she said. "I remember it well from my youthful days of poetry and wine beneath the bough. There was this one time when this boy, his name was Herc Gabriel, took me out to Winnow's creek ..."

"Hey!" said Cynthia. "Back to the poem."

"Fine," huffed Ruby. "If you don't want to hear about Winnow's Creek. It's perfectly clear. Sara Teasdale? *The Song of Solomon?*"

"Oh, *my*!" said Meg, understanding registering on her face.

"What?" said Pete.

"It's a love song," said Meg. "*La Chanson d'Adoration* is a love song."

"For Henry," said Ruby. "It was a love song for Henry."

"What do we do now?" I asked, once the pizza arrived. "It's a conundrum. Musically, this last movement is what the cantata needs. It's the way that she wrote it and it makes perfect musical sense. But *with* it, the whole thing is a love song. If we leave it off, there is certainly every argument to be made that it is, or could be, an Advent or even a Christmas piece."

"We could go ahead and finish with *I Wonder as I Wander*," suggested Pete. "You know, this revelation is last minute and all. No one would blame you."

"I don't think I can do that," I said.

"I don't think you can, either," said Meg. "I think Rhiza has to sing the last movement."

Rhiza's eyes widened. "I don't know ..."

"Sure!" said Cynthia. "I've been sitting next to you in the choir. You have a wonderful voice."

"You *have* to do it," said Meg.

"Agreed," said Pete.

I looked at Rhiza and she shrugged. "Let's make a copy of it at the church when we're done," she said. She pointed her finger at me. "Then you and I are going to go over it. If I'm going to sing it, I'd better learn it first."

Chapter 18

Sunday morning was windy, but not too cold. Christmas Eve. Meg and I drove down the mountain and into town, marveling at the natural beauty that surrounded us: pine and fir trees dotting the otherwise barren hills, frozen waterfalls shimmering on the rocks, even a black bear lumbering across the road ahead of the car. Meg's John Rutter Christmas CD was in her stereo and we *Holly and Ivy*ed it all the way to church.

The morning service was good. The hymns were good, the choir was good, even the sermon was good. Father Ward Shavers had been rising to the occasion as of late. The church was full, but that was normal on any Sunday this close to Christmas. An even larger crowd was expected for the evening service. We sang Niles' Appalachian carol, praised the Lord, and everyone had coffee after and came away refreshed in the faith.

After church on Sunday, I spent an hour recopying the English horn and organ parts into something a bit more readable. Rhiza and Will, the English horn player, met me at the church at 9:30, a half-hour before the choir was due to arrive. Edna Terra-Pocks was already at the organ. Marjorie was upstairs, too, always early, and this night, very excited. She'd brought Henry, the bassoon player, with her and by their laughter, it was obvious that they'd been to a few pre-service Christmas Eve soirees.

Rhiza sang through the final movement with the instruments accompanying her. When she finished, none of us said anything. Even Marjorie was silent.

"That's that last thing Bessie was talkin' about yesterday?" Marjorie said finally.

"That's it," I said.

"We're not singing that wandery song again, are we?"

"No, we're not," I said. "We are certainly not."

"Good," said Marjorie.

At ten o'clock the loft was full and the choir's excitement was palpable. It took several minutes to get them all into their seats, their music into their hands, and their mouths closed. I went over the music for the communion service, just so everyone knew what would be coming next, and then we turned our attention to the cantata.

"Are we singing *I Wonder as I Wander*?" asked Cynthia. "What's the verdict?"

"We have the final movement from Miss Baker," I announced, "so we're not singing the carol."

"I hope it's easy," said Bob. "We don't have a whole lot of time."

"It's a solo," I said.

"Really? A solo?" said Muffy, hopefully.

"Yep," I said. "Rhiza will be singing it, accompanied by Will on the English horn, and Edna."

"Humph," said Muffy, obviously miffed.

"They've already rehearsed," I said. "Everyone will be seated after the fourth movement, and we'll listen to the ending with the congregation."

I hadn't quite finished my announcement when two unexpected figures appeared in the back of the choir loft, standing at the top of the staircase. One was Pauli Girl, and the other, leaning on her arm, was Miss Bessie Baker. I stopped talking and stillness filled the church. One by one, the choir members turned to follow my gaze, and as they did, they saw the old English teacher just inside the doorway.

Pauli Girl, obviously embarrassed at the sudden silence, said, "Miss Baker wanted to come up." She held one of Bessie's hands and her arm was around the fragile woman's shoulders, supporting her as best she could. Bob Solomon jumped up to help.

"Thank you, Robert," Bessie said, motioning him to sit down. "It's nice to see," she paused to catch her breath, "... that you finally learned some manners," she paused again, "... after all these years." She waved him away. "Take your seat. I'm fine."

But she was far from fine. Bessie Baker had made it up the stairs to the choir loft with Pauli Girl's help, but now she was white as a ghost, and struggling to catch her breath. She held up a frail hand, fingers splayed, and took a long moment, waiting for her discomfort to settle.

"I just want to say," she started, but then her voice caught in her throat. She coughed, and began again. "I just want to say that yesterday's rehearsal was the most moving performance I've ever heard. Not because the music is mine, although I am very proud of it, but because you all are performing it so beautifully. Thank you."

We all sat, dumbfounded.

Her tone changed. "I'll be listening in the back. Don't you dare give me any less than you did yesterday!"

"No, ma'am," said Pete.

Chapter 19

There had not been a Christmas Eve service like it in the history of St. Barnabas. Everyone said so. The cantata went as well as it ever had, maybe better. Father Shavers was at the top of his game. The choir sang, the congregation sang, we had communion, lit candles, and joined together singing *Silent Night* at the end. It was the service of everyone's collective memory, whether they owned that particular memory or not.

When the congregation finally left the church to make their way home, they were greeted by a breathtaking, snow-covered landscape. The flakes had started falling an hour earlier, and they were still coming down. The moon, full and bright, hung above the bare trees of Sterling Park and bounced her light off the alabaster landscape, illuminating the square in a soft, blue-white glow.

"It's beautiful," said Meg, hanging on to my arm as we surveyed the town square from the double doors of the church. "The service was beautiful, too." We walked down the steps and onto the snowy path. "The whole thing. Beautiful and wonderful. I won't ever forget it."

"I won't, either," I said.

Pauli Girl McCollough called to us from across the square. We waved and she came across the park, stepping carefully so as not to slip on some unseen snow-covered ice. She was wearing an old coat, one of Ardine's I thought, and had a scarf wrapped tightly around her neck. We waited for her beside Meg's car.

"Merry Christmas!" Meg called to her when Pauli Girl was close enough to acknowledge her greeting. "Did you take Miss Baker back to the nursing home?"

Pauli Girl didn't answer, but walked up to us and threw herself into Meg's arms.

After several minutes, Meg gently pulled Pauli Girl away and looked into her eyes.

"She died," Pauli Girl sniffed. "We stayed and listened to the cantata; then I drove her back and we were sitting in her apartment talking. About fifteen minutes later, she just closed her eyes and stopped breathing. The doctor said that it was her heart."

"Oh," said Meg, obviously startled by the news. "I'm sorry."

"I was hoping she'd make it to Christmas, but she didn't."

"I didn't know she was that sick," I said.

"She never acted like it," said Pauli Girl. "But the doctor told me that he didn't think she had more than a couple of weeks, and that was back at Thanksgiving."

"Well, you took good care of her," I said.

"Know what? Right before she died, she smiled at me and said, 'thank you.' She never did that before."

"Just before midnight," said Meg. "We sang her cantata and she got to hear it. That's what she meant. That's what she thanked you for."

"I don't know if I'm cut out for this nursing stuff," sniffed Pauli Girl. "What if everybody that dies affects me like this?"

"Then you're doing your job," I said.

Chapter 20

She found herself at the top of a mountain, her mountain, standing on the rocky promontory jutting out over the valley, a place she'd been hundreds of times. Snow blanketed the world and was still falling. She noticed that, although she was in her nightgown, she wasn't cold, and she'd been cold for so very long. She looked up at the moon, a shimmering sphere of silver, then let her gaze fall across the ranges that appeared as blue-green silhouettes of varying hues, row upon row, before disappearing into the smoke that gave the mountains their name. She was contemplating the scene beneath her when she felt a hand slide into hers.

"Hello, Henry," she said, without looking.

"Hi, Sweetpea. That was something, that music. I always knew you had it in you."

"It took so long," she said. "So many years." She turned to him and smiled. "I've missed you, Henry."

"I've missed you, too."

She was quiet for a minute, then looked back into space and said, "It was for you, you know. That cantata. It was your Christmas present. " She sighed and added softly, "But you never came to get it."

"I know it was, Bessie. A wonderful present. Thank you. I'm glad I got to hear it."

"I'm glad, too."

They stood and looked out over the clouds hanging in the hollows of the hills. A million remembrances raced through her consciousness, but disappeared as quickly as they came. Finally, when the images had passed, and her mind was quiet once more, there were the mountains. The mountains and

127

the moon and the snow and the music—music surrounding her as she hadn't heard it since she was a girl.

It swelled and circled and swept over her like a wind. She closed her eyes and breathed it in.

"Are you ready to go?" he said finally.

"I'm ready."

He kissed her then. "Merry Christmas," he said.

"Merry Christmas."